From the River's Edge

From the River's Edge

Elizabeth Cook-Lynn

Arcade Publishing • New York

Little, Brown and Company

FIRST EDITION

This is a work of fiction. Smutty Bear, Struck-by-the-Ree, William S. Harney, Zephier Rencountre, and Long Mandan are historical figures. Some of the places are real and some of the events are historical, but any resemblance to living persons is not intended by the author and is coincidental. (Portions of an actual trial transcript appear in the narrative, though places, events, and names have been changed and fictionalized.)

The author gratefully acknowledges the following publications in which the poems in this book were first published: *The Greenfield Review:* "The World He Lived In," and *Then Badger Said This:* "The Last Remarkable Man."

LIBRARY OF CONGRESS CATALOGING-IN-PUBLICATION DATA
Cook-Lynn, Elizabeth.
  From the river's edge / by Elizabeth Cook-Lynn. — 1st ed.
    p. cm.
  ISBN 1-55970-051-3
  1. Dakota Indians — Fiction. I. Title.
  PS3553.05548F76   1991
  813'.54 — dc20   90-47258

Published in the United States by Arcade Publishing, Inc., New York, a Little, Brown company

10 9 8 7 6 5 4 3 2 1

MV PA

Design by Barbara Werden
Published simultaneously in Canada by Little, Brown & Company (Canada) Limited

PRINTED IN THE UNITED STATES OF AMERICA

Contents

Preface

Seeing the Missouri River country of the Sioux is like seeing where the earth first recognized humanity and where it came to possess a kind of unique internal coherence about that condition.

As you look you think you see old women leaving marked trails in the tall burnt grass as they carry firewood on their backs from the river, and you think you hear the songs they sang to grandchildren, and you feel transformed into the past. But then, winter comes. The earth freezes solid. And you wish for July and the ripe plums and the sun on your eyelids.

One August day I stood on a hill with Big Pipe and watched the flooding waters of the Missouri River Power Project unleash the river's power from banks which had held it and guided it since before any white man was seen in this country. As old Pipe grieved, the water covered the trees of a timber stand which had nourished a people for all generations, and it took twenty years for those trees to die, their skeletons still and white. It took much less time for the snakes and small animals to disappear. Today, old Pipe has a hard time finding the root which cures his toothache, and he tells everyone that it is the white man's determination to change the river which accounts for the destruction of all life's forms.

When you look east from Big Pipe's place you see Fort George; you look south and see Iron Nation, and you sense a kind of hollowness in the endless distance of the river span, at odds, somehow, with the immediacy of the steel REA towers stalking up and down prairie hills. Yet, as your fingertips touch the slick leaves of the milkweed and roll the juicy leaves together, it is easy to believe that this vast region continues to share its destiny with a people who have survived hard winters, invasions, migrations, and transformations unthought of and unpredicted. And even easier to know that the mythology and history of all times remains remote and believable.

Part One

A Trial

Issues of Law as Well as Fact

Smutty Bear

"I am an Indian, but the man then told me I would become an American. To do this, he said, my son, what you have to do is to take care of the white people, and try to raise two or three streaks of grass. I have tried to do this, and have worn all the nails off my fingers trying to do it. Ever since I have tried to raise that corn, and I am still at it, but can't raise it."
(Translation)

Summer 1856

1

August 1967

The lawyer came out to Tatekeya's place along the river that day.

He said to Tatekeya: "This is not about your stolen cattle, John. It is about justice and the law, as are all cases brought before the United States bar."

"But what's the chances of gettin' my cattle back?" asked John.

"Well, we don't think in terms of getting your cows back or getting paid for them, necessarily. We think in terms of what is *fair*."

Very quietly and with mixed emotions, John answered that he thought the two things, i.e., the return of his stolen cattle and *fairness*, were one and the same.

"Not necessarily," he was told.

2

He stood in the cluttered, stuffy little kitchen, looking out of the narrow window, stirring the bean soup boiling in a pot on the gas stove, and absently watched the wild turkeys mince toward the brittle weeds along the dirt road, their small heads jerking up and down as they pecked at fallen seeds, their beady eyes alert for any quick movement. A suspicious kind of bird. They stepped prettily into the trees, disappearing quietly as John's thoughts rambled.

He was glad his wife, Rose, had moved to town with their married daughter, giving him the opportunity to live by himself for the first time since their marriage thirty years ago. His was now a solitary, thoughtful life, as he had, perhaps, always wanted it to be.

A tall man in his early sixties, a man who had been nurtured on the prairielands of the Dakotas but one who showed little evidence of that hard life, John Tatekeya had black hair imperceptibly streaked with gray, his face was unwrinkled, the delicate, fine bones of his profile were strangely sharp, unburdened by the passage of time.

On this day, the kind which began with a morning so cool and bright as to seem extraordinarily bountiful, he lost himself in private thought, absorbed in the precious moments like this that he shared with no one, secretly and selfishly savoring his own feeling of insularity.

It was an important morning, but soon the heat from the stove in the small three-room house would become unbearable, he knew, and the sun would climb into the sky, and his clothes would get so damp they would hang limply about him, and he would be sucked empty of energy and vitality by the muggy, shimmering air. And he would cease to move about with such spirit. Only those born into the hot, dry Dakota winds of August ever got to know how to really thrive in it. The others simply tolerated it.

The tall man at the stove seemed untouchable and remote at this moment, as he meticulously spooned the thick soup into a bowl, turned off the gas heat, and seated himself at the bare table. He ate silently, methodically, taking great care in breaking the salty crackers and dipping them slowly in the mild liquid. When he was nearly finished, he sugared his coffee generously and sat stirring with quick, short strokes, holding the spoon palm-up. He looked through the gauze curtains at the hayshed, a recently moved and converted trailerhouse, corrupted by the dispassionate sun and relentless prairie wind long before it was moved to John's place.

Tacky.

Makeshift.

Cluttered and distracting.

He lifted his eyes toward the hills which spread out and away from the river, like earthen monuments of the past, forever, ophidian, resolute. John did not give much thought to himself as a man of the north prairies. But he was as much that as are the men of the other prairielands known to the world — the men of the pampas of Argentina, the llanos of the South, the steppes of Eurasia, the highlands of Africa, and the tundra of the Arctic. Like them, John Tatekeya of the Dakota prairielands and his people had forever possessed great confidence in their collective presence in their homelands. More than he thought about it, John felt it and simply held it in his heart.

As his eyes scanned the windswept hills he knew this: It is here that the spirit himself can *wokeya. Wo-ki-ca-hni-ga-to?* Didn't Benno say these things when he talked to them in the sweatlodge? His crying sometimes helps human beings, Benno said. But not always. What can I do now? men have eternally asked, and John Tatekeya was no different. What can I do now, he asked also.

The wind bent the tall grass to its will, brushed weeds haphazardly across the roads. Even the birds seemed frail in its grip as they lifted their wings and dropped across the sky.

Minutes passed, and John sat at the little round table in the bright stillness, mixing, cooling, stirring his coffee with quick, short strokes. Finally, he lifted the bowl to his lips and quietly drained it. He stood up and reached for his hat just as he heard heavy footsteps on the front porch.

He stepped outside, slamming the door shut quickly.

"Hau," he said, smoothing his hair down with one hand and fitting his Stetson on with the other. He shook hands with the young man from the Federal Bureau of Investigation and pretended a graciousness he did not feel.

"You ready, John?" asked the young man, whose red hair almost matched his flaming cheeks so recently burnt by the August wind which never ceased to blow across these prairies and hills at this time of the year.

"Yeah."

U.S. government agents, or "FBI men," or *"wasichus,"* as Tatekeya now thought of them, were nothing new to this Indian reservation in recent years. Nor were they absent from the other Sioux Indian homelands in South and North Dakota. The joke used to be that in every Indian home, there is the mother, father, children, grandparents, and the anthropologist. In the sixties, that joke changed to include the "G-man." Figures of almost unrestricted federal law enforcement activities had a long history on Indian reservations, beginning even before the passage of such legislation as the Major Crimes Act and other "congressional violations of Indian Nationhood," as John described the white man's law of the nineteenth century.

The theft of John Tatekeya's cattle occurred just about the time when groups of young American Indian men began to patrol the streets of urban America. Streets like Franklin Avenue in Minneapolis–St. Paul, where men in red berets would resist police violence toward "relocated" Indians and participate in a variety of activities which were soon to become the substance of a full-fledged political movement called "Red Power" and "AIM," claiming national and international attention.

Before John's case would go to trial, the American Indian Movement would be full-blown, and people all over the world would know the meaning of "justice" in Indian country. And because of the controversial nature of the activities in urban America during this period, the rural, reservation, so-called trust lands were also under FBI surveillance in ways that they had not been since the late 1800s. It was then, John's older relatives had told him, that the Department of War/Interior police force was placed on most of the reserved lands in the country, a colonial law-and-order force which changed Sioux justice for all time. Though he thought of himself as essentially a law-abiding man, these facts of history indicated to John the presence of some kind of alien force on Indian land that was at one and the same time coercive, obligatory, discordant.

The federal agent with the flaming cheeks who appeared at Tatekeya's door this day seemed innocent and somehow frail. John walked beside him to the government rig, which had THE DEPARTMENT OF THE INTERIOR, U.S. GOVERNMENT stamped on both its doors. John peered into the slats of the shiny blue and silver trailer, checking on the saddle horses, which were nervous and stamping and blowing dust from their nostrils.

John, who had been, "just for the hell of it," a rodeo saddle-bronc rider in his earlier days and even now considered himself an expert horseman in the tradition of the great Sioux centaurians of the past, looked with quiet suspicion at the mares which had been brought to his place from the Agency pastures.

"You think these old gov'ment nags are gonna make it?"

"Just a minute, John," said the young man, laughing. "They're pretty fair examples of fi-i-ine horseflesh!" But he, too, peered into the trailer, as though to either confirm or deny John's assessment.

John shrugged and got into the rig.

Together the men and the horses would conduct a futile search of the long-grassed hills of South Dakota and Nebraska for forty-two head of John Tatekeya's cattle, stolen months before, all of them carrying the ID (Indian Department) brand.

3

As they pulled away from John's place, they looked sideways at the large tipi at the rear and the small house in front, both set apart from a recently planted grove of elms and oaks to the west, the large corral standing in the tall grass, and a couple of outbuildings blazing in the morning light. Red Hair, unaccustomed to the rough, rutted reservation road, drove carefully and slowly. The house, looking like someone's bad joke, was set up on blocks, the front screen door was hanging ajar, and the front steps were detached from the stilted porch. There was no foundation under the house, but electrical lines had recently been connected and John had begun to have hope.

The pickup pulling the horse trailer moved laboriously from the scene.

Along the road, wind had blown clumps of weeds into the barbed-wire fences, which held them there. And more were piling up. By late fall the fences would be so clogged with thistles a jackrabbit couldn't get through. It became a metaphor in John's imagination for his own struggle, and he silently watched a small whirlwind sweep dried leaves and weeds in its path.

The wind knows how to do things to interfere in the lives

of men, thought John, and Dakotahs have explained to themselves the significance of its power through various means. His mother had resisted it all, having been persuaded finally by the simplicity of Christian beliefs to give up the complicated and difficult worship of the Four Winds, and he himself, because he had been her favorite son, was also dissuaded to some extent from practicing the old ways.

"Si-i-i-lent ni-i-i-ght, ho-o-o-ly ni-i-ght" rose incongruously in John's memory as he watched the thistles being swept before the wind. He remembered himself as a child of seven standing first on one foot in the bitter, sweeping snow, and then on the other, then entering the church singing Christmas carols and holding candles, which acolytes set ablaze as each communicant entered. He had looked over at his mother for approval and she had smiled at him, and her smile would forever haunt him. This Christian way was less time-consuming and easier on the physical self than any of the Indian religious practices John had come to know, and it had been a comfort for both of them and an assurance that everything was all right. He had believed that until his mother's death when he turned nine years old. It was only at her graveside that he was faced with the fact that he knew none of the important songs which would assist her journey into the next world.

He thought of the ease with which they had been persuaded to believe in the white man's religion, and as the pickup truck driven by Red Hair made its way down the graveled road and out of the bend in the river, John put the memory of his mother out of his mind, pulled his hat down over his eyes, and pretended to sleep. Now at sixty years of age he knew that the white man's law was no more powerful than his religion but just as pervasive, and he decided that he would try to pretend that this trip with Red Hair was something more than a futile gesture. It was, after all, the best they could do at this time, and it might lead, eventually, to the truth about who the men were who committed this crime against him. He had to find the truth and get his cattle back.

The horses in the trailer grimly held their positions as the government rig pressed southward, Red Hair talking and chewing gum with equal vigor and John silently musing about his own culpability concerning the theft, which had cut his herd nearly in half.

"I betcha some one of your neighbors done it, John," said Red Hair. "Who do you know who doesn't like you? Who needs money?"

That's just about everybody, thought John, though he didn't raise his head nor did he answer. He really didn't want to enter into this discussion; he considered it small talk, that chatter designed just to fill up the empty spaces which he had begun to realize were intolerable to the white men that he knew. Though they taught in their Sunday school classes that silence is golden, none of them that he had become acquainted with could stand silence. This young man, he decided, was a real talker. Liked to hear his own voice.

Sorrowfully he turned his thoughts to his own recent behavior. He had been drunk and absent from his place for nearly two weeks and was told later that he had been seen in Presho, Chamberlain, Pierre, even as far as Sturgis and Rapid City.

"They've been sold piecemeal, John," Red Hair went on, totally oblivious to John's unresponsiveness and now warming up to his subject enthusiastically. "And we're gonna have to get on these horses and ride some of those ranches down there and see if we can identify any of your stuff.

"You know, selling them piecemeal is what a cattle thief will do because it makes them harder to trace that way," continued the younger man with his one-way conversation.

Yeah, thought John, and if the government and me don't find my cows we're probably gonna come to the end of our bargain, ennit, Red Hair?

As the Department of Interior rig pressed on through the grasslands of western South Dakota and emerged into the endless Nebraska fields of cornstalks, dry and brittle from the August winds, John began to wonder about the issues at hand and thought that they might not be as simple as they seemed to be at first glance.

John had been one of the few men in the district to qualify for the government "payback" cattle scheme. The U.S. government provided you with fifty head of cattle, for example, and you paid them back with your calf crop for the next thirty years. He still had his own allotment, he had over the years purchased the allotments of his brothers and sisters, and so he was considered an Indian landholder who could be assisted to financial security through a federally funded cattle ranch project. John had always run a few cattle. It was the way he and his father and his brothers had always lived in the contemporary world. But in the middle of a booming postwar economy it was thought that Indians ought to become big cattle ranchers. Run cattle for profit. Enter into the free-market economy of the greatest democracy in the world. John was one of the first to be contacted by the agent to apply for the funds.

He'd been at it now for three years along the Missouri River, in the midst of a time of great confusion and upheaval during the harnessing of the river for hydropower, the building of several huge dams (one of them near Pierre the largest rolled-earth dam in the world), and the subsequent flooding of thousands of acres of Indian land.

Some of John's own land was now under water, as were the lands of his neighbors. In the middle of this confusion, John had to ask himself, What kind of man is out to ruin me? Who among my neighbors would do this thing and why? I know them all and have known them all of my life; I've worked and boozed around with them, prayed and grieved with them in times of sorrow; shared their joys and triumphs. And now I am getting to be an old man. And this, now. Just at this time. Who?

No, he thought, it must have been outsiders, men who are unknown to me, strangers who have crept in to steal a man's livelihood without compassion, men I don't know, men to whom I am not related, and, therefore, men without conscience.

This was John's hope, but the depth of sadness in his heart acknowledged that his hopes might not be upheld. He might never know the answers to the troubling questions he now posed, and even if he did find the answers, they might not be the ones he would want to hear. He might never see his cattle returned, which not only would be a loss of great magnitude, financially speaking, but would also serve as a reinforcement of his secretly held notion that the world in which he now lived, the modern life which he tried to be a part of, unconnected as it was to his past, was cruel and without honor.

We Dakotahs used to know how to live, he thought. But they told us to settle down, and become like them. This is not the world in which we can steal the horses of the Pawnee, and they ours.

Ah, well. . . . The four wires of his fence had been stretched and held to the ground, he knew now, and a couple of large trucks had driven into his pasture, up to the corral and loading chute, and more than forty head of John's one hundred and seven horned Herefords had been loaded out. John had one of the best and largest herds on the reservation, the envy and pride of everyone around. His relatives could come to him now and expect that he would feed them. He gave meat for the feast at every summer dance, and he was known throughout the country for his generosity.

It had probably taken three or four men to do the job on a moonlit night, and silent and unnoticed, they had probably driven down this same isolated road, John mused.

Regretfully, John recalled the agony of his own recalcitrant behavior, and he could think of no excuses. He had driven into the barren yard nearly two weeks after the theft, looked around for reassurance though he knew that Rose would not be home, and petted his big hound dog as it emerged from under the front porch. John had felt nauseous.

He was red-eyed and aching from too much liquor and too many nights laid out in the bed of his pickup or slumped behind the wheel.

He'd gone into the house and sunk tiredly into the over-stuffed chair for a few minutes before he headed for the bedroom. He slept for a couple of days, thinking that if he stayed in bed the dizziness in his head would stop, but it only seemed to get worse and it caused skips in his heartbeat every time he stood up. He couldn't eat. Before he could get better, he shuffled outside and went around to the back of the house. Shaking and weak, he had started the fire to heat the stones for the sweat he knew he needed.

Later, he had gone from pasture to pasture, at first driving his rig because he felt so weak; the next day, he'd saddled the old buckskin gelding and ridden slowly through the bottomlands near the river looking for any telltale tracks. He did this for days not knowing what else to do.

One late afternoon, after such a search, he sat in the saddle smoking a cigarette, and when he looked up into the sky he noticed perched in a nearby cottonwood a silent, handsome owl keeping watch over his activities. As he moved along the subirrigated eighty acres, he felt on his neck the old carnivore's gaze.

"That old man," he said under his breath. *"A i sta wa hna ke sni"* (why does he not take his eyes off me?). He turned in the saddle and hollered irritably, "Get the hell outta here!"

John found himself wondering about this owl, sitting there in a kind of ineffable quietness that was disturbing, turning its head toward him since its eyes, set immovably in their sockets, could not change their positions, purposefully keeping track of his movements. He felt it to be less innocent than many of the species known to him, and he wondered what it knew.

Some owls hunt night quarry only, John thought. Those

were the kind with eyes on each side of the head so that they seem not to be looking in the same direction at the same time. And since it was getting late in the afternoon, John at first thought this owl keeping watch on him might be one of those.

But it was not. On the contrary, this owl, which had become John's attendant, however briefly, in this matter, seemed to be one of those splendid companions of prairie dogs known in this country to exist for the purpose of maintaining the balance of nature in other than obvious ways. Yet it was too large to be one of those burrowing owls, those tiny creatures who run about prairie dog towns on long, spindly legs. It was huge. Magnificent. And John rode on, thinking, and listening, and holding the reins taut, the old gelding's prancing gait forcing him to stand crouching in the stirrups.

Uninterested in violence, disconnected from the natural urge to strike out, this owl seemed ageless, and John began to imagine that it might even be one of those said to have accompanied the people on their migration into this world. Was it not, though, a hunter? What was it hunting? It seemed not to be trying to frighten those who inadvertently came upon it. John was, if not frightened, at least startled by its persistence.

Even as his horse swung gracefully into the tall grass along the river's edge, and as he bent over the saddle to look for signs of the movement of his cattle, John had the feeling that there was nothing here worth searching out, nothing that would answer the question of the whereabouts of his cattle. And the presence of the handsome bird seemed to affirm that feeling.

Looking over his shoulder, John watched the great bird's silent flight to another tree, where it perched higher, with its toes placed so that there were two in front and two in back. It detached itself a second time, and then another, its hush wings lifting it toward the highest tip of a huge cottonwood. From that vantage point this bird of prey stared into the fading light, and John kicked his horse in the flank and they plunged on and went away.

When he reached the road which wound its way into the bend of the river, John again put the spurs to the buckskin and rode hard and fast back to his own corral. He would have to seek answers elsewhere.

4

"*Ti ma hed hiyu,*" said Clarissa graciously. Harvey Big Pipe's elder daughter greeted her father's old friend John Tatekeya at the door, and she gestured for him to come in.

The rooms smelled of meat and onions; a clutter of tinted photographs of children and young men and women, some of them in military uniform, hung on the walls. A large curtainless window overlooked a backyard filled with old cars, "junkers" everyone called them, except when they were in need of something, anything from bolts and brackets to carburetors and drive shafts. Then they were called valuable resources for auto parts and taken seriously. A black-and-white charcoal sketch, carefully hand-framed in black plastic, of the infamous Santee chieftain, Little Crow, was propped up behind the radio on a makeshift shelf, and a long braid of sweet grass, burnt at both ends, was carelessly draped over it. Caked white paint peeled from the windowsills and doorways, and the scrubbed linoleum covering the floor glittered in the afternoon light.

"Are you looking for my father?"

"Yes."

"He's not feeling too good," she said softly as she offered John a chair.

John sat down, and when Harvey came slowly from his bedroom, John asked about his health and was told that he was feeling better. The conversation consisted mostly of complainings about old men's ailments, starting out as a discussion of a serious nature; and it went on and on, one man's story told to best the other, one story getting more obscene than the next, until all the family members who had begun to gather in the room, even Clarissa, who usually feigned shock and embarrassment at hearing these kinds of stories, were laughing good-naturedly about the willfulness of old age, the instability of a body hesitating, wavering, hemming and hawing, no longer possessing the strength to do what was asked of it. Then John was asked to stay for supper.

After the meal and as the two old friends smoked, John began to talk seriously of his ordeal, saying what everybody knew, that he had forty-two head of cattle missing.

"I walked that subirrigated eighty acres along the river but saw no signs," John told his old friend. "I even saddled up the old buckskin for another look but I didn't see no signs.

"Just then," he continued, "I decided that I would come over and see if you had heard anything."

"No. Nothing," he was assured.

John went into great detail about the recent signs inside the narrow pathways of his pasture corrals and around the loading chute and the tire tracks which had been nearly obliterated by the hooves of the remaining cattle.

"I finally had to admit to myself," John told Harvey, "that cattle thieves was on my place, and then I went to the Agency and I filed papers. Me and that FBI man, you know, that one with the red hair, we've been all over looking for them," he said, gesturing widely.

"We even went to Ainsworth. All in all we found three with ID and my brand on 'em. And there's another one that I know is mine but the brand is gone.

"But, I've still been looking," he continued, "because over forty head is missing.

"I just don't know where else to look," he concluded.

Big Pipe said nothing, merely shaking his head and offering his condolences.

When John left the house and walked to his pickup truck, darkness had fallen. He saw one of Harvey's sons, who had been chopping wood, walk slowly toward the barn and tack shed carrying a lighted flashlight. The light, yellow and gloomy, swayed about the foreboding outlines of the buildings and abruptly disappeared. John felt a strange uneasiness as he drove slowly home.

5

It was in the last days of September that John parked his International pickup truck at the curb and walked across the immaculate lawn, still green in spite of the fall chill, surrounding what was called the Federal Building in Pierre, South Dakota, where the trial was to be held. He looked at the cars parked along the curved street and hoped that he wouldn't see Aurelia's old Dodge among them. She didn't say she was coming and he hadn't asked her not to, but he hoped that she would not.

John's experience with the law was considerable. He had been hauled in by the police many times. The tribal police, municipal cops, the state patrol. Driving under the influence, speeding, resisting arrest, illegal parking, no license tabs, assault. You name it. One time when he was too drunk to get his pants zipped up after he took a leak outside the Silver Spur in Fort Pierre they even booked him on indecent exposure charges.

"Hey, listen to me, officer. This is a big mistake. I'm not . . ."

"Shut up, chief. We gotcha."

So he had a sheet on him as long as his arm, and it didn't

look good and he wasn't proud of it. He'd gone to court many times. Always "guilty as charged."

Though facing up to it was nothing particularly new for John, this time the tables were turned. He was the guy bringing the charges. He and the Feds, that is. And he didn't know exactly how he felt about it — a bit apprehensive, if the truth were known. On the one hand, he needed to get his cattle back or get paid for them; on the other, he had no real assurance that any of this would turn out all right. He alone faced the white lawyers, the white defense attorney, white prosecutor, white jury, and white judge. The FBI said it was on his side in this matter, but he knew enough about the FBI to make them seem more unreliable than they owned up to.

Inside, he went up the white marble stairs to a desk where a tall, large-boned, graceful, and dignified white man sat, checking in the participants for this awkward meeting, Indians and whites coming together to testify for or against, telling the truth or making up lies for the "jury of peers" to see who is more believable than the next, like pawns in a chess game of legal mumbo-jumbo where John's rules for survival no longer applied. A game, for Indians at least, which had its origins in the not-so-distant past, it was an ongoing and consistent fraud, set up to make all of those concerned believe that justice in Indian Country was real. But such games seemed totally oblivious to the presence of historical duplicity in any particular case. The white man has always stolen from the Sioux, he thought as he climbed the stairs. First it is our land, then our way of life, our children, and finally even the laws of our ancestors. And now this white man, the son of my white neighbors, has stolen my goddamn cows.

John approached the desk. The white man's chin was covered with the hairs of a short beard which hung straight down in vertical streaks of black and gray, and his dark mustache was clipped short. His forehead was smooth and white and it sloped back into a receding hairline of limp, brown hair combed thinly to one side. His blue eyes seemed kindly, his mouth soft, uneven, expressing a shyness next to obsequiousness.

John looked him over and unaccountably tried to imagine who he was. He saw a man with probable Czech peasantry in his lineage, one of those often derisively referred to as "bohunks" out here in the West where there was a corrupted myth that ancestry hardly mattered; a scion of those peasants who had determinedly and valiantly resisted fascists in Middle Europe for generations then became fascists themselves in the new country. They now found themselves living supposedly quiet and nonviolent lives, yet undeniably, in John's view at least, lives of imagined conquerors with fully implemented laws of their own making, transplanted into the midst of a relentless and unfathomable indigenousness virtually unknown to them and therefore unacknowledged.

The bearded man looked solid, somehow official in his casual, expensive plaid shirt, his fingers and thumb making circles of airless discontent as he went about his paperwork. Those who knew him thought him to be the kind of man who was fond of talking about people with "lots of dough," for to have great wealth was a major objective which he held out for himself, and he took note, usually, of those who might serve as examples of these values he held.

Certainly, as he tentatively faced John Tatekeya, the Dakotah whose cattle, it was alleged, had been stolen by one of his white neighbors, he dismissed him as anyone who could measure up to his private dreams of success. He faced a man who was from the Indian reservation, which, for the bearded man, was light-years away from his own life, and the Indian exhibited none of the criteria necessary for consideration. The bearded man might have been among those in the community who had already made up their minds about this case.

Disdainfully, the bearded man asked John to spell his last name. T-a-t-e-k-e-y-a, John said slowly. Then he pronounced it. Tah-TAY-kee-yah. When the bearded man did not respond, John pronounced it a second time. John knew he was supposed to feel unworthy in the man's grand presence, like a miscreant of some vile order as the man wrote the name down and shuffled papers on his desk. But he didn't. It only made a tacit hostility rise in his heart, and he silently watched the circles of the man's left fingers and thumb turn to broad stroking, like the dusting strokes of a cleaning woman on the smooth varnish of the table. On his left hand the dignified man wore a heavy, square ring of glittering, ornate Black Hills gold. He wrote with his right hand carefully and quickly, an air of efficiency and pretentiousness pervading the room.

Unexpectedly, the man yawned and his teeth were very white.

"Sally went over there several times," said a woman's sharp voice from the rear of the room, the shrillness dissolving into a murmur of muffled sounds resounding oddly into the huge ceiling, an empty, hollow sound.

John Tatekeya watched the nameless blond woman and the efficient, graceful white man writing his name in a book and yawning. There was nothing here to bring cheer to John's thoughts as he began to feel that his case, the business of trying to get his cows back, only cluttered up a system preoccupied with much more important matters. His worries were made insignificant by a world which had long since dismissed him as merely troublesome and his way of life as unworthy. He began to understand that the theft of his cattle was neither life nor death to anyone here but himself.

He sat on a wooden bench in the hallway to await the arrival of his lawyer, the District Attorney who wore cowboy boots and tried Indian cases for the federal government now and then, a man who prided himself on being an amateur historian on the life and times of General George Armstrong Custer.

Born in New Haven, Connecticut, to Quaker parentage, the lawyer now, after twenty years in the Northern Plains, took on the attitude and historical perspective of a place which had been only in the imagination or fantasy of his childhood, and John recognized immediately that the two of them had little in common. The DA was a man who, much like his neighbors, acted on these private fantasies.

"Most of what we know about the Custer battle at the Little Big Horn," he began eagerly when he met John that morning to decide on the details of the trial, "is based largely on the work of General E. S. Godfrey.

"You know," he went on enthusiastically, "Godfrey wrote quite a bit on this as early as 1892." He was blissfully unaware that John was not even remotely interested in this kind of information. Godfrey's account about Custer, as far as he was concerned, was the white man's history. Not his.

What's shaping up here, thought John as he waited in the courthouse, leaning his arms on his knees, is a big waste of time. Half of my herd is gone and I am probably not going to get them back.

He and the redhaired FBI man had ridden their horses for a week through the pastures where it was thought the cattle might have been taken after the illegal sales. They found three head with his brand and the ID brand on them, one at Irene, another at Highmore, and one at Ainsworth, Nebraska. There was another steer that John knew was his but it could not be officially identified. That's what's left of my forty-two head, he thought sadly.

"Shit," he said into the empty hallway.

Waiting.

The waiting seemed interminable.

Often, when he was a kid, he had sat with Benno in the blind, waiting. And together they had waited for the Canada geese to settle on the glaring ice and eventually waddle ashore where two or three of the honkers could be picked off with Benno's old 12-gauge. John remembered this now as he sat on the wooden bench in the courthouse, and he thought of it in retrospect as the kind of childhood activity in which there was no such thing as failure or guilt.

The solutions to life's problems often seemed clearer under these kinds of circumstances, John knew, and so they had become activities which he had carried over into his adulthood. Now, John clasped his hands together in a nervous gesture of desperation.

"Old Hunka of the People," he thought to himself:

your scarred breast
grows soft and translucent
   in blue-gray photos
on the wall in oval frames
   hidden under dust
a man to be remembered
   your ancient tongue
warms men of fewer years and lesser view
   you tell of those who came
too busy fingering lives with paper
   to know what they can't know
they liked the oratory
   but thought the case was hopeless:
go home, old Benno,
   it loses something in translation
drink the wind and darken scraps
   of meat and bone
stars won't rise in dreams again
heads bent
   to clay-packed earth
we smoke Bull Durham
   for bark of cedar
but know
   in council, talk's not cheap
nor careless in its passing
   the feast begins with your aftervision
we speak of you
   in pre-poetic ritual.

His wish at this moment was that he could go back to those days when Benno was showing him how to survive and that such survival was possible. He remembered that they would quickly pluck the soft feathers from the underbelly of the goose and from between the legs, and then they would stuff the plumes into the buckskin bag, paying no attention to the blood and the limp neck and the latent death twitches which often took place as the plumes were gathered.

The aging Benno, breathing hard from the exertion, would

drop a smooth black stone into this buckskin bag, say his prayers, and walk slowly through the heavy snow the three miles to his house, which was situated on a hillside away from the river and the wind. John would follow along, bearing the dead goose in anticipation of the family feast. Benno would carefully place the bag in an old brown mahogany dresser with his clothing and other articles he used in ceremony.

John tried to make sense of why this "aftervision" of Benno was so much on his mind lately. He could not say why that was so, and even after the trial was over and for the rest of his life he continued to carry with him the ever-present memory of the old man. Perhaps it signaled some kind of change as he grew older, a reconsideration brought about by age. Perhaps it was because the old man in every gesture, in every word, in every action had restored the ethical nature of how a man might live in this changing world, and John could not let go of that.

Whatever the reason, John knew, now, sitting in this white man's courthouse, despairing over the loss of his cattle, that this kind of ethical influence was reserved for certain others like Benno, not for himself. But when he thought about how he was going to make it out of this life, he began to wonder, facetiously at first, if he was going to have to become celibate as Benno had in later life, giving up women and booze and the "good times." He continued to regret that the events of the past months did not make him look like a man of honor. He was, after all, responsible to those who depended upon him to be good and upstanding. And his recalcitrant behavior was inexcusable. Not knowing what message for the future was possible, he accepted the fact that his lands were flooded and his cattle were missing. More significantly, he accepted the sorrow of the loss of Benno, of the old man's companionship that had, in retrospect, meant everything to him. Thus, the memory of the old man continued to be everywhere around him, indelible, profound.

Even though John did not speak his name and had not heard it on the lips of those around him for a long time, he knew that he was not alone in the belief that the old singer was one who, like Smutty Bear and Little Crow and Gray Plume and the others, had seen the shadows moving near and had warned them. He had been among those, John thought now, who had been moved by the power of the gods, toward wisdom and freedom. Too late, perhaps. Too late.

6

Testimony: Day One

October 1967

District Attorney Walter Cunningham: "Well, now, Mr. Tatekeya, do you know whether or not you sold any cattle from the first of that year, 1966, up until the time that this count was made by the officials?"

A: Yes. I sold some cattle last year.
Q: Last year?
A: Yes.
Q: Was it before or after this count was done by the Credit Association?
A: It was after.
Q: I see. Well, did you sell any cattle before the count was taken?
A: It was after.
Q: I see. Well, did you sell any cattle before the count was taken? In other words, from January 1, 1966, to this April date when you made the count?

Mr. Joseph Nelson III, attorney for the young white man accused of stealing Mr. Tatekeya's cattle, at this point in the trial stood up slowly, and as though the whole process had already become loathsome and tedious to him, he said, "Again, your honor, I'm going to object to these leading questions. Now . . ."

The judge, Mr. Niklos, turning toward the younger attorney in an attitude of apology, said, "Well, now, let's remember, first of all, this witness is, as he says, an Indian. He is halting. I'm not entirely sure how readily he understands the English language. I'm not placing him as a reluctant or a hostile witness, but I think we do have to consider his education, his background; and I am going to rule out questions that suggest the answer, but I am going to permit the United States Attorney to ask questions that may be somewhat leading for the reasons I've just given you.

"Overruled.

"Now," turning to the clerk seated a few feet away from him, he said, "would you read the question again, please."

Clerk: Did you sell any cattle before the count was taken? In other words, from January 1 of 1966 to this April date when you made the count?
A: Yes. I sold cattle before the count was taken.
District Attorney: When was that?
A: Well, that was sometime during the fall; later part of the summer or early fall.
Q: Well, what year would that have been?
A: That would be last year.
Q: The latter part of the summer or early fall of last year. Is that right?
A: Yes.
Q: Well, Mr. Tatekeya. Maybe you don't understand quite what I am getting at. Now, last year was 1966. Is that right?
A: Well, last year is when I sold them cattle.
Q: OK. And you say that was in the summer or fall?
A: That was in the fall, I'd say.
Q: In the fall. Well, now, what I'm getting at, you said that you sold cattle in the fall of 1964. Is that right?
A: That's right.

Q: And that's the only bunch of cattle you sold in 1964. Is that correct?

A: That's right.

Q: And you said, I believe, that you didn't sell any cattle during 1965.

A: That's right.

Q: Now then, did you sell any cattle from the time that you had these missing cattle — that's in the fall of 1965 — up to the time that you made the count in April of last year?

Before John could answer, the young defense attorney got to his feet. Indignant now and anxious to show the jury how he and his client were being wronged, he shouted, "Just a minute, Mr. Tatekeya!" and he waved his hand menacingly toward John on the stand.

Turning toward the judge, the attorney for the accused, his face beginning to redden in resentment, said plaintively, "Your honor! Sir! I would like to make a standing objection here. . . . This can't be allowed. . . . This cannot go — "

"You may have a standing objection," answered the judge quickly. Then, looking down at the papers on his desk, he continued:

"I call your attention to a United States case of *Antelope* vs. *The United States,* an Eighth-Circuit case, in which you have an Indian whose testimony is somewhat halting, who was a little hesitant and had difficulty in understanding all of these legal matters, and where it appears necessary to ask leading questions to get the material facts involved. Now, I'm not going to let the U.S. Attorney testify or put words in this man's mouth, but I think that he is somewhat confused on dates, and because of the fact that he is Indian, I am going to permit leading questions."

"Well," said Mr. Nelson III grudgingly, "just so it is understood that — "

"You may have a standing objection to all such questions," interrupted the judge. "Now, the minute it reaches the point where the District Attorney is doing the testifying instead of the witness, you call my attention to it and I'll sustain your objection, probably, because I'm not going to permit leading questions."

"Well, I believe that to be the case right now, your honor. That's why I made the objection."

"I don't believe so," said the judge. "We have to get the material facts out here." He looked at the lawyers, scanned the courtroom. His head down, eyes peering over the rim of his glasses. The wise old man. Fair. Judicial.

To the clerk, he said, "Let's hear the question again."

John, during this exchange, sat with a controlled, sullen look on his face, his elbows on the armrests of the great wooden witness chair, his large hands hanging loosely. He knew he had only a limited capacity for what he considered to be phony, self-serving behavior, and anyone who looked at his face knew that his tolerance for it was being strained.

It doesn't take too much brains to know what is happening here, John thought. The defense attorney's legal maneuvers are being used simply to distract people's attention (especially the jury's attention) from the accused, and I, myself, am now the focus of suspicion. What about the wheels of justice, white man? Are they turning forward or backward? What in the hell . . . . ? He was not confused, now he was angry.

Before, when they tried me for being drunk or driving without a license I deserved to be treated like crap. Not this time, *wasichu*. Not this time. In the white man's court, though, there is no difference between the guilty and the innocent. All the same. That's what they call equality, ennit?

A faint smile touched John's lips as he looked up and saw the bearded, yawning sentinel, the man from the outer hallway, carefully opening the heavy, polished door to the courtroom. That guy, thought John. He just can't quit.

The doorkeeper came inside and tapped a woman seated in the third row on the shoulder. He motioned for her to follow him and she did so. The door swung silently shut and John turned his attention back to the business at hand.

John looked at the cowboy lawyer and wondered at his naïveté. He really believes in this, he thought. He really thinks he is winning the case. But that should be no surprise. In all cultures and in all times, people have made laws in which they have found faith and in which they have found self-affirmation. People have always found processes of thought and modes of reconciling conflicting considerations. Certainly, the Dakotahs have done this for longer than is known.

John's thoughts got more specific. It does not matter to this "good" white man, John said to himself, it doesn't matter to this cowboy from Connecticut that everyone here is casting doubt upon me in the process of the trial. It doesn't matter that he has to make me look like a fool in public as he "defends" me. He sees no contradiction.

It's kind of like those book-writing men who come out here to the reservation, John mused, and they ask the people all kinds of questions, write everything down, and eventually go away to write their books in which they tell lies about us. There was one scholar who came here to Fort Thompson and Crow Creek, John remembered, and he passed out cigarettes to everybody and we all stood around smoking and visiting with him, being polite and entertaining as is our custom these days to a stranger, a visitor who didn't seem to know much about us. And then, just recently, just a few months ago, my youngest daughter brought that book home with her from college and in it this white man wrote that we had no toilets, sometimes didn't even bother to go into the trees to urinate, and that we really didn't care what kind of meat we ate. *Tado,* he said, was our only word for meat and we didn't make any great distinctions about it.

I should know better by now. Indians like myself should probably avoid participating in such white man's doings. And we should avoid trials and courtrooms. I should know by now that the white man's notions about these things are almost always in direct conflict with what my people know to be ethical.

Only rarely have I known the Dakotahs, John thought, to

seek truth by victimizing the aggrieved one. And when they have done it, everybody has known that it was not a part of the institutionalized process of legal reasoning and ethical base of our cultural survival; that it was behavior unsanctioned by our elders and therefore unprincipled. Dakotahs have always had confidence in their own lives.

I, too, must have confidence in such things, and, of course, I still do. Some people who have lost faith in the old ways have begun to think of Old Benno, our teacher, when they think about him at all, as just an old windbag.

But I do not. It is widely believed among us, John thought as he sat waiting for the questions to be asked that everyone knew the answers to, that we must not dehumanize our opponents in the process of seeking the truth. Else, the truth becomes meaningless. To legitimize such a thing would allow anyone to accuse anyone else of the most outrageous crimes and to be forever after in doubt. And here I am. By implication, accused. Of an outrageous crime. Stealing from myself and my own family. Everyone who knows me knows that, since I have become an old man, my pride in myself would not allow me to do such a terrible thing.

The court dialogue resumed.

"Now, then," read the court clerk in an expressionless voice. "Did you sell any cattle from the time that you had these missing cattle — that's in the fall of 1965 — up to the time that you made the count in April of last year?"

A: Uh . . .
DA: Now, take your time, John. . . .
A: (*long pause*) I, uh, sold some cattle.

Looking about the courtroom, he felt everyone's eyes on him, and he began to feel the burden of rising paranoia. How careful need he be here? What were they accusing him of? No. No. He wanted to protest. I am not the accused. Why . . . ?

John wanted a cigarette. Was there no end to this tedium? As he looked around he saw two of the Big Pipe brothers,

Jason and Sheridan, seated in the courtroom in the spectators' section. His own wife, Rose, was sitting just behind the
railing, and he worried again, for just a moment, that Aurelia
might show up and it would be embarrassing for everyone
concerned. Perhaps he should have cautioned her.

The little courtroom seemed unusually packed and stuffy
at the beginning of this little trial, the first day of the official
proceedings. People were even standing in the back of the
room, arms folded, shifting the weight of their bodies from
one foot to the other, shuffling, whispering. John's apprehen-
sion momentarily diminishing, his thoughts gave way to his
own curiosity. He cocked his head and lifted his eyebrows
and wondered, almost contemptuously, of what interest this
foolish little trial could be to most of these spectators. Didn't
they have anything better to do?

Only as a last resort was this whole thing something that
John had considered appropriate. He had always held to the
traditional belief that Dakotahs living on their own lands
should handle their own affairs in their own way and that
the federal government's intrusion into these matters was not
only foolish, it was clearly illegal.

And now, endlessly answering these tiresome, repetitious,
dangerous questions, he worried that his decision to join the
United States government in this legal matter against a white
cattle thief on Indian reservation, "trust" lands might not
have been a wise one.

What had the United States government ever done for
him? John had asked himself before entering into this
agreement. Did it ever protect the lands of my grandfathers?
Did it ever come to the aid of those who wished to practice
our religions and teach our children in the old ways? No. On
the contrary, he answered himself silently, it was an accom-
plice in all of the thefts historically suffered by my people.
John felt certain that it would be again the white man's way
which would turn against him, an Indian.

That was the way of history. Why, then, did John participate in what he viewed as a corrupt system of justice? Many
years later, when John was very old, blind, and nearly deaf,

he would still pose that question, and oddly, he would continue to answer it in a way which one could only see as an effort to explain the ambiguities of his existence to those who still loved him and surrounded him in a protective and familial circle.

Private solutions and individual decisions about matters of this kind, John would concede, were not always possible, regrettably, nor were they definitive. This explanation did not, of course, exonerate him, but at the same time, neither did it condemn him.

So he would tell a story or two:

Story #1

"To be an allottee and a citizen of the United States," the agent told Benno, who stood before him holding a form letter addressed to him from the Bureau of Indian Affairs, Washington, D.C., "you must do what it tells you in that letter."

"No."

"You must choose your allotment."

Benno took out a huge handkerchief, wiped his face, and paused.

"No, thanks."

"You must choose your allotment."

"No. Sir."

They stood staring into one another's eyes.

Later, the agent chose the allotment for Benno and registered it in his name.

"It is way up the Crow Creek, somewhere on past that little white man store up there. Way on up there," the protesting Benno told everyone, his arm flung out in a wide gesture.

"Taskar and them live up there, but me and my family have never lived there. We don't want to live there. There's too much trees there along the ridge and it gets too dark in the winter."

He got another letter in the mail telling him he was an allottee:

Each and every allottee shall have the benefit and be subject to the laws, both civil and criminal, of the State or
Territory in which they reside.

Benno had said no again, and for the last time. He never
again spoke a civil word to the agent. And he sent the letter
back by his eldest daughter, who lived at the Agency. He
continued to live along the *sma sma* creek where he had
always lived. And when the agent and his secretary came to
"talk some sense" into the potential but recalcitrant allottee
and citizen, Benno took a few warning shots at them with
an old .30–.30 he kept by the front door. He shouted at
them in Indian to go away.

"Han sni! Hanta wo!"

Benno was declared "incompetent" by the Department of
the Interior at the request of the agent very shortly after this
hair-raising event. The agent, after all, was an ex-school-
teacher from Sioux City, Iowa, who had taken up government service because there was more money in it, and he was
not, he would tell you in no uncertain terms, accustomed to
taking gunfire from crazy Indians.

The allotment which bore Benno's name, then, was put
up for sale eventually by the agent who was acting "in his
behalf," and a white man from Pukwana who raised pigs
and turkeys purchased it.

Story #2

Eddie Big Pipe, Harvey's younger brother, rode over to
the "squaw man's" place and shot fifteen head of prime, fat
hogs. He did it because the white man, married to a tribal
woman and living on her land, would not keep them away
from Ed's watering place along the creek.

Big Pipe had paid dearly for the individual action he had
taken upon himself. There had been no further dealings between the two antagonists, and the Bureau of Indian Affairs
officials at the Agency ever after that looked upon Ed as a
troublemaker, one who was unreliable and dangerous.

In defense of this admittedly astonishing behavior, Eddie Big Pipe had later made a joke of it.

"Well," he would say in mock seriousness, "I could have shot *him!*" and everybody always roared with laughter.

Some others in the community, however, the "squaw man," his wife and her relatives, and, especially, the Bureau of Indian Affairs officials, were not amused. Seeing no humor in the situation, they avoided Big Pipe, and when they could not avoid him, they glared at him from a distance.

Tatekeya used this story to discuss the ideas of justice as they applied to Indians, and he always gave the impression that shooting the "squaw man" might not have been such a bad idea.

7

Except for wise men and the colonized, almost no one pays attention to the fact that history repeats itself. Though John Tatekeya may have considered himself neither wise nor colonized, he was, nonetheless, a man who knew his own history. He saw the ironies inherent in the historical relationship which his people had long since established with the invading whites; sometimes he was entertained by it, oftentimes dumbfounded, and always appalled and uneasy.

Just across the river from where he sat in the witness chair in the federal building, in this crowded courtroom testifying in a legal process which seemed to be directed toward the improbable notion that he had himself stolen his own cattle and was now falsely accusing a young white man of the crime, one of his grandfathers, Gray Plume, had once attended a great Council meeting where nine tribes of the Sioux Nation had met with the white man soldier William S. Harney. Even at the time that it occurred, in 1856, all of the people had recognized that they had been ordered there to defend themselves from the accusation that they were thieves by the very people who were stealing the Sioux homelands.

True to his grandfather's memory, John now sat in quiet contemplation of those events of a century past and, in his own silent admission, concluded that what had happened at the Harney Council was known to have happened over and over again and was happening at that moment.

Sometimes, John thought, it takes only a small event in the life of an ordinary man to illuminate the ambiguities of an entire century. I know now, at last, finally, John reasoned, that the council which Harney directed all those many years ago must have been very much like this one, that it is the white man's thievery which is legalized and the Indian's behavior which is made criminal in either case. It is always a part of the strategy that the white man's whim must be satisfied and that he must be made to look fair and decent. Reasonable. Compassionate.

John Tatekeya was beginning to understand why he was a cynical man.

"The Council lasted many days," the grandfather Gray Plume had told everyone, "and Rencountre, the half-breed Frenchman who was the Sioux language/English interpreter, worked very hard to make sure that there were no misunderstandings.

"It was very clear what General Harney wanted," said Gray Plume afterward. "He wanted all Indians removed and he wanted Indians to obey his law. He wanted all Indians who were said to have committed murders to be delivered to the nearest military post so that the white man, not Indians, could decide upon their fate; and, more important, perhaps, he wanted all Indians to stay away from the roads traveled by whites.

"In our own land," said Gray Plume, "we would forever after that be told where we could go and where we couldn't, who among us must be punished and how we must punish them. Hang them. By the neck with a rope. This, we think, is barbaric. And the Sioux have never administered justice in such a manner."

Gray Plume had listened carefully, and he had heard many things which influenced his thinking from that time on. He had heard Zephier Rencountre interpret endlessly for the officials:

> Indians must not obstruct or lurk in the vicinity of roads traveled by the whites [and] certainly Indians must not molest any travelers through their country.

In response to it all, Gray Plume, a man who had a good understanding of the meaning of reciprocity, had wanted to ask, "And what is the obligation of those visitors and travelers to our land? Are they blameless? Right? Guilty? Innocent? Poor? Rich? Who are the thieves here?"

Well, thought Gray Plume. We are accused, often, by the white man who knows a thing or two about thievery.

What are they doing here? Who are they? Tourists? Sightseers? Explorers? God's men or the devil's? Gold seekers? Do they not possess their own homelands? Will they let us go into their homelands and settle there as we please?

He had wanted to ask all of these questions, but, of course, he did not. In the retelling of the event it was clear that he had not then, nor in the rest of his long life, received an acceptable answer to these tacit inquiries.

The observation is still made by those who examine history, and it was certainly made by the grandfather Gray Plume, who had witnessed these particular events, that great forces had clashed on this continent and the old order for each was changed forever. It was clear to John that Gray Plume had understood what had happened, thus he never questioned the old man's interpretation: that from the very beginning there must have occurred a vast release of energy, unequaled in the experience of North America, and it manifested itself in a compelling behavior pattern of interaction which would forever plague Oyate, the people. It was clear to John, as it had been to his grandfather, that the thousands of years of life force and occupancy by the Sioux upon this land would be from that time on at grave risk.

Whenever Gray Plume spoke of these historical matters, he made it clear that it had seemed to him the zeal with which the white man soldier Harney, the Christian missionaries who preceded him, and the justices who followed pursued their own goals was surely unique. To be sure, Gray Plume had given little thought to the apostolic age which had inspired such behavior in the so-called new world, and so it was left him to ponder alone the conception of justice which the Council articulated, just as it was now left to the grandson John Tatekeya to wonder about his lawyer's purpose, the motives of those in the courtroom.

Though John was now past sixty and was just in these late years beginning to understand the consequences of former times, the grandfather Gray Plume had been only twenty-six years old when he attended this Council and learned these things. Very early in his life, then, Gray Plume had become a man to whom the people listened, and his influence, surely, continued throughout his life.

Whenever the grandfather told and retold his remembrances of the Council's deliberations, he philosophically speculated that if the Dakotapi were to survive the modern world, they would have to recognize that the religious views which brought about what he regarded as the eminently unfair system of justice for Indians in America promulgate in their followers the notion that a righteous good father may be displaced by identification with Jesus Christ. And that displacement, Gray Plume reasoned, was what allowed men to become gods themselves.

"It is a dangerous way," he would say.

This became Gray Plume's view, and he had many, many relatives.

Gray Plume, like an Ancient Mariner of the North Plains doing penance, went about repeating word for word the Harney oration delivered to the nine tribes, which was forever in his memory:

Now, listen to what the Great Father says: first, that all Indians who have committed murders, or other outrages upon white persons, shall be delivered up for trial to the commander of the nearest post; second, that all stolen property of every description in the hands of any Indians shall be restored to its rightful owner, for which purpose the chiefs must be responsible that it is taken in without delay to the nearest military post; third, that Indians must not obstruct or lurk in the vicinity of roads traveled by the whites, nor in any way molest a traveler through their country.

Gray Plume warned that Harney was a powerful and vicious enemy of the people and that their lands and ways were under severe attack.

The grandson John Tatekeya, now in a modern court of law participating in a way of justice condemned by the ancients of his people, looked into the eyes of those in the courtroom and knew genuine hostility. What is the meaning of a man's history here? he raged silently.

Since the days of Gray Plume's attendance at that Council, moralists have argued that the sanctity of international ethics was clearly under fire during those proceedings, but on this day Tatekeya himself was momentarily at a loss for words. Was he the only one who saw that it was useless for him to have to come here and defend himself and his honor? Was he the only one who knew of Gray Plume and remembered his warning?

Tatekeya could not shake from his mind the drama which had been witnessed by his grandfather. He could not rid himself of the image of the old man doing penance for his mere presence at the Council and for his very participation in such historical events. The old man's final and oblique interpretation of it all which rang in his ears now had made him forever sad:

"In the previous year to this Council, my relatives," Gray Plume had said, "Harney himself had massacred the Sichangu at the Blue Water in Nebraska."

The old man had always feared that he would not die before the theft from the people of the sacred Black Hills would be, finally, legitimized by the white man's corrupt law; that the white man would say to his people, you can get along without your life, because I have mine; that an unjust world would make it impossible for his grandchildren to live just lives.

Nonetheless, he made his annual pilgrimages to the significant mountain in those hills that would forever bear the enemy's name, not only because he was a holy man, but because in his dreams he was welcomed by the winter scent of the pine trees, the soft rumble of thunder in the summer rain, and the reverberating flashes of orange and blue lightning upon the darkness of the land.

Finally, sometime after the turn of the century and just before the first great war in Europe, Gray Plume had gone into the next world, his irreconcilable fears unappeased.

8

Testimony: Day One

(Continued)

October 1967

Q: Let me repeat the question, Mr. Tatekeya; when did you sell these cattle?

A: (*pause*) Well, unh, I sold some cattle last fall, and then this fella come out this spring to check my herd.

Q: Well, Mr. Tatekeya, last year was 1966. Is that a fact or isn't it a fact?

A: Yes. That is a fact.

Q: Now, is it correct that you say you sold cattle in the summer or the fall of last year, 1966. Is that right?

A: Yes, that's right.

Q: Now, these here missing cattle that you testified to earlier. That was in the fall of what year?

A: 1965.

Q: All right. Now, from the fall of 1965, then go on through the winter months of 1966, the first part of 1966, January, on up to April of 1966. Did you sell any cattle during that time?

A: No.

The District Attorney, with considerable relief showing in his face, looked toward the judge as if to say, "You see? We did get to the right answer, didn't we? Between the fall months of that year and the spring, when the cattle were missing, he didn't sell any cattle!''

The lawyer's face expressed both pain and triumph.

John looked at the lawyer and thought, But there was never any evidence that I sold cattle during that time. There were never any receipts, no checks. Nothing was ever presented as evidence for the accusation that I sold my own stuff.

Nonetheless, the lawyer seemed jubilant that John had at last uttered the appropriate words, that he had not sold his own cattle, that he seemed, now, to be an honest man whose cattle were indeed missing and that he had nothing to do with it.

"Fine," the lawyer said to no one in particular.

Everyone in the courtroom seemed to understand, too, that a milestone had been passed and that John had finally given the right answer, and there was the sound of feet shuffling and the clearing of throats following this long and confusing exchange.

John looked into the faces of the members of the jury, the spectators. Did they really think that I stole my own cattle? Do they still think this? Do they believe that I would accuse a man falsely? I wonder if their doubt will still linger long after this trial has ended and that, when this is all over, people will still think I'm a liar.

The young white woman who was married to Sheridan Big Pipe got up from her seat during this brief pause, sidled up the aisle, and started toward the door, tiptoeing so that she would not disturb the proceedings. John watched the backs of her heavy, white legs, mottled with the blue-gray shades of varicose veins, propel her toward the exit. Her purse flapped noisily against the side rails of the spectators' seats, and Sheridan glared at her retreating figure. Her conspicuous behavior called attention to Sheridan's presence, and John again was puzzled by his interest in this theft and trial.

What is he doing here? John wondered. This does not

concern him. And his family has already declared to me that they know nothing about the theft or the whereabouts of my cattle.

He turned again to his lawyer, who was smiling brightly at him.

"Fine," he repeated.

"Now," said the lawyer, drawing in a breath, "now, Mr. Tatekeya, when you noticed your missing cattle during the fall of 1965, do you know what kind of cattle you were missing?"

"Sure."

"What were they?"

"Herefords."

"Well, now," said the lawyer uncertainly, "well . . . I mean . . . what were they? Steers? Heifers? What?"

"There was eight cows and eight calves, eight yearling steers, and eighteen yearling and two-year-old heifers."

The judge raised his hand and said, "Just a minute. Just a minute. I'm sorry. I didn't get all of that."

The clerk, also taking notes, said, "I didn't get it all either. Let's hear that over again."

The judge turned to Tatekeya. "Would you say that again, please?"

John said very slowly: "Eight cows." (Pause) "Eight calves." (Pause) "Eight yearling steers." (Pause) "And eighteen yearling and two-year-old heifers."

He glanced over at the court officials meticulously recording the information as though this was the first that they'd heard of it.

More in sorrow than in impatience or anger, John looked down at his feet. His Tony Lamas needed polishing. He should have polished them before coming to the courthouse this morning. Oftentimes, Aurelia sat on the edge of the bed and polished them for him. Chatting comfortably. Her round shoulders glistening and soft. He wanted to apologize. He wanted desperately to see her.

9

The commitment John now had to Aurelia had started simply enough, perhaps. A diversion, he sometimes alibied privately and in retrospect: at first, an embarrassed admission that the physical nature of a twenty-year-old marriage might not be enough for his sexual appetite. He even went so far as to suggest to himself that the striking young woman's love for him eased the pain of his middle-aged life, made him feel less agony because of the upheaval of the last ten years. When he had been forced to move his cattle, his home, and his outbuildings out of the way of the backwaters of the hydropower dam called Oahe, one of several such federally funded dams forced upon the Missouri River, he felt great despair.

He saw his mother's allotment, those of all her brothers and sisters, the Poor Chicken land, the Walker and Howe and Shields allotments, and many, many more disappear under the great body of water; thousands of acres of homelands all up and down the river which had nourished the people, now gone. Cemeteries and Christian churches were moved out of the way of the flood at the last minute, and cottonwoods, elms, and ash trees which had stood for hundreds of years along the banks of the river turned white with decay as their roots were swamped. Nothing survived the on- slaught. The medicine roots and plants, the rich berry and plum bushes, the small animals and reptiles, were swept away, trivial sacrificial victims of modern progress.

And the world was again changed forever.

"What is happening, John?" his wife asked one day when she returned from hunting the *ti(n)psina*. "It has moved and now I can find it nowhere. Do you think that it has disap- peared for good?"

John didn't know how to answer her.

That spring, which seemed to signal the dam's completion, when the disaster had somehow come to a point of no return, when most of the people had moved out of the way of the incoming water, Tatekeya's small house had also been moved, across the small rise in the land to the draw about four miles away from the river. There was no time to move anything else. And for years after that he had none of the promised electricity, no fences to hold in his cattle and horses, no water except the ever-seeping backwaters, no barns for storage, and no haystacks to feed his stock for the coming winters. It was a time when his wife nearly gave up, a time of great stress, waste, and confusion.

One day, he had taken Rose to town for a brief visit with their grandchildren, and upon his return home he attended the peyote church meeting which had been hastily arranged as a grieving ceremony for the death of one of Aurelia's young cousins. The people of the community wept together and prayed for the restoration of health to everyone. They ate the sacred food. And when the meeting was over, John had walked to his car with Aurelia. He had taken her into his arms as though he were a penitent. Humble and touched.

From that time on, self-conscious and bitter, he had loved her.

When they entered the large room, they saw an array of narrow beds, and all of them were filled with the skinniest, most wraithlike bodies that John had ever seen. It looked like something from the war, like the pictures that you saw in the newsreels.

The air in the room was nauseating; it reeked of the human odor which was the aftermath of bodily functions performed in a limited space. The smell hung like death in the windowless rooms and remained trapped in the high ceilings and closets. John was sickened. He felt inept, clumsy, and useless. He had never been good in sickrooms. In fact, when his wife, Rose, underwent a gallbladder operation at the government hospital years ago, he had not been able to bring himself to visit her there. He had instead sent his sister in his place and later suffered pangs of guilt for seeming to be uncaring.

Everywhere he looked, there was an array of rumpled bedclothes and frail, skin-and-bones men whose lives had brought them to this imperfect place to mend or to await release, whichever came first. John had been instantly thankful that Benno had avoided this long and relentless kind of decay which can precede a man's exit from this world. Benno had simply gone to sleep one night and never awakened. On this day, as he surveyed the scene of human misery, John didn't know whether to laugh or weep.

He felt Aurelia move toward the nearest bed, and as she approached her beloved grandfather, John knew that he needn't have worried about how he could help her. She simply knew, instinctively, how to love and comfort the old man to whom she had been devoted since infancy.

"Grampa is going to get better," she had told John as they were driving to the rest home. And now that she was here, she behaved as though that were a certainty.

"*Tunkashina*," she shouted into the bony, hollow face of the old man, whose deafness was becoming more profound with every passing day.

John could tell, almost instantly, that the old man did not recognize her.

"It's me, Grampa." She took his bony hand in hers.

"It's Aurelia."

Startled and afraid, the old man, lying with his mouth

open, lifted his head a few inches from the pillow and stared.

"How are you?" she asked in a loud voice, ignoring what John thought was fairly obvious, that the old man was, to use a phrase from his catechism days, right on Jordan's banks.

There was no answer from the old man.

"Are you OK, Grampa?" She was nearly hollering now.

Still the old man did not speak. She waited. Then she leaned closer, and suddenly lowering her voice, she moved in and leaned toward the old man's ear. "*Toniktuka he?*" she asked softly.

She waited for him to look directly at her.

Hoarsely, the old man repeated the question: "*Toniktuka he?*"

Bewildered, he looked at her searchingly, trying to remember who she was, his dark eyes clouded, the pupils empty. John, standing beside her with his arm at her waist, thought for a moment that she was close to tears.

". . . relia . . . *wicincina*," the old man whispered pitifully, recognition finally breaking through his mental confusion.

His withered hands began to feel around the bed for his cane, moving the bedsheets this way and that, until Aurelia grasped his wrist and held his arm. With just a little pressure she got him to lie back down, and then she started to talk to him as though everything were all right.

"You don't need your cane, Grampa. You can't get up right now. OK?

"Look, Grampa," she said. "Look. I dug some wild turnips. . . . They're really hard to find. . . . I dug them a while ago with that stick you made for me. Do you remember? Look. They're really good. See? I hung them over the stove to dry. These are some of the smallest ones. Here."

She lifted up his head and put a huge pillow under his thin neck, and he was pushed into a forward position like an old, wrinkled turkey thrusting out its skinny beak.

Aurelia took no notice of his awkwardness.

"Here's one, Grampa." She handed him a small turnip.

"They're pretty dry, ennit?" she shouted. "Just suck on it, hunh?"

Then she put one in her own mouth and chomped hard on it.

She smiled into the clouded eyes.

As the old man tried to get enough saliva in his dry mouth to suck on the tiny turnip, John nearly burst out laughing. The gracelessness of old age and the innocence with which Aurelia confronted it seemed suddenly outrageous and sad. Obscene, yet humorous.

Oblivious to the hilarious spectacle of the toothless old man's effort to comply with her wishes, Aurelia began talking about the old times. She told him conspiratorially, "It got dark and the coyotes had to leave me on my own," sharing with him an old story they both knew.

Tucking in a blanket at the edge of his narrow cot, she asked, "Do you remember that, NaNa?" calling him by the childish nickname she had given him when she was just an infant and barely able to talk, trying to share with him now the old story which held some of the secrets of the irretrievable past they both had known and he, for the moment at least, no longer remembered.

An old man from the next bed, startled out of his daze by all of this activity in this ordinarily silent room, rose from his pillows like a graying Lazarus and shouted to no one in particular, "I'm fine! I'm fine! *Oh-ha(n)* . . . yes!! I'm doing OK," and then lay down again as though in slow motion.

A tragicomic scene, thought John, touched by the pitiful nature of these final days, still half-amused at this disconsolate drama of unblest senility. He sat in the big, orange, leatherlike chair beside the old man's bed that day, and even though he knew that the old man would have been angry at his presence, he had stayed: compelled, somehow, to be with Aurelia as she made her duty-visit to the old grandfather now living out his latest illness in the new tribal rest home.

John, like the old grandfather, had become an appreciative listener of Aurelia's. And even when she was drunk and behaving contentiously, as she sometimes was, he was always reassured by just the mere sound of her voice. He noticed that she had the ability to adapt the rhythm of one language to change the sound of another. And so, when she talked in English she often used the sounds of Dakota, the cadence and tone of Dakota speech. This day, he sat and listened to the cadence of her voice, and in his own heart he knew that what it amounted to was a kind of purity of speech, an attempt on her part to retain some of the sense of Dakota aesthetic in everyday life. And it always seduced him in ways that he could not completely explain.

He sat and listened to her work her spell on the old grandfather, and he wondered how long it would be before she would do these things for him, no longer a lover, merely a nurse easing the life of an old man, caressing his dry forehead, speaking to him as though to a child. The thought filled John with dread.

The difference in their ages had only lately begun to be an issue between them. The last time they had made love he had covered her breast with his hand, put his lips to her neck, and whispered, "You will find someone else one of these days, Aurelia. Some young man. And you won't be able to catch your breath. What will I do then?"

She had only smiled. And her touch was cold.

10

There had been rumors about Aurelia since anyone could remember. That was because men had always wanted her. Even when she was twelve, still long-legged and sallow from a sick childhood filled with hardships, men were drawn to her beauty. Some of her growing years, when she was not attending a boarding school or living at her grandmother's place, she spent in a three-room house abandoned by the U.S. Bureau of Indian Affairs employees who no longer wanted to live forty miles from the Agency, a house which had been built across the road from a Catholic church and a cemetery at a time when the services and religions of white colonizers were brought in to create the center of a little community adapting to an enforced relocation and agrarian lifeway.

Because of her beauty, Aurelia was watched constantly. Her grandmother, in particular, took it upon herself to open her eyes to the realities of the kind of life she thought Aurelia could count on if she were not relentlessly compelled to duty. This was the child who had been given to her in infancy, the child who would have the responsibility from birth to be the companion of her grandmother. Such a child, it might have been said by others who had greater insight, should not

---

have been given also the responsibility of great beauty, for the contradictions of living in such a way are often overwhelming.

Such girl children who are meant to accompany the aged are ordinarily plain and docile, and because Aurelia was neither, her grandmother's suspicion became the very attitude which nurtured intolerance and accusation. It was her grandmother who first noticed that men wanted to put their hands on this youthful beauty, and she reported it to the sisters of the child's mother. From then on, every action of Aurelia's was noticed and commented upon, and her natural tendency toward vibrancy and joy was taken to be the sign of recalcitrance and mischief.

The home in which she spent some of her years prior to womanhood had three rooms, one for cooking, the second for eating, and the third for sleeping and loving. As a consequence of these circumstances, Aurelia was never innocent. She had never been one of those protected children forced into speculating about the mysteries of sex. She had never had to wonder nor fantasize about what was done between men and women in the night, for she grew up listening to the words and sounds of passion. She grew up knowing that for her parents, grandparents, uncles and aunts, married sisters and brothers, cousins, and all who slept in that long, narrow room making love, quarreling and relenting, weeping and laughing, this momentary and transitory offering of human passion was the best that could be expected. The family members who functioned as her role models were, in her view at least, frail and needful. Early on, then, she "played around" as a kind of quiet resistance to all this, and she began to indulge the men who sought her. Early, then, the gossip had started.

By the time she was almost a teenager, she seemed already mature, already an adult. And when the grown men returned in 1945 from Germany and Japan and the Pacific wars, her family, because there were many daughters of marriageable age, received special invitations to the "honor dances" for returning warriors. It was expected that she too would put on her finest clothes and dance and, sooner or later, make the choices that her sisters had made in finding suitable husbands.

But she did not. She had become contemptuous of those young men who wanted to bring her things, and she became the kind of young woman who, for reasons known only to herself, drove away those who might have comforted her, even frightening them so that they began to watch her from the corners of their eyes.

She continued to accompany her grandmother. Some of the time they lived along the Crow Creek and sometimes in the breaks of the Missouri River country where her father ran cattle. From her grandmother's little house along the creek they could take a footpath to the flat prairie above and worship in the Christian way at the gray Presbyterian church, which faced east in a clearing surrounded by tall prairie grass and wildflowers. Grace Mission, an Episcopal church which stood as evidence that the missionaries of these various Christian faiths understood the jealous spirit in which they competed for the souls of the natives, was not far away. It was to the Presbyterian church, however, where Christian hymns were sung in Dakotah language every Sunday, that Aurelia took her grandmother and sat beside her to share in the warmth of the wood-burning stove in winter and in the oppressive heat in summer. A winding road led to the Agency, past a small hill, past a dry creek which also, at one time, fed into the Missouri River.

One Sunday evening, Aurelia and her grandmother left the potluck dinner being served at the Presbyterian church to join their relatives gathering in the Indian way to console one another on the loss of a young man of the community who was a cousin to Aurelia. An army corporal, he had been shot by unidentified persons in Korea on the eve of his departure for the States, and the grief that this unexpected death bore into the community was profound.

The old lady and Aurelia walked in the sunset to the gateway and entered the house of the young warrior's parents, shaking hands with those seated on the floor along the walls.

The singer began, his voice deep in his throat. Later, near the edge of sobs unuttered, deep agony in every hard breath he took, he sang of the story which told of his gift and how he must share it with the people. Aurelia sat, unmoved, and it was only when her grandmother unexpectedly began to talk that she straightened her shoulders and tried to listen: slumped near the wall, the old woman told of petting the she-buffalo when she was an infant, and how it had followed her, and when she turned around, her infant tracks were blue.

"You must guard the sealed doors of the room," Aurelia heard someone say. "Don't let his power out."

The men lifted the singer off his feet and held him.

Much later, a drummer started to sing as the morning light dawned, and the others joined in:

> *wana anpa'o u we yo*
> *wana anpa'o u we yo*
> *wana anpa'o u we yo*
> *wana anpa'o u we yo heyana he de do we*

Exhausted and spent, the singer sat on the mattress on the floor in his room and changed his clothes.

His new wife put pans of food out for the worshippers and mourners, and Aurelia began to carry the bowls into the outer room. She sat next to John Tatekeya and ate heartily, and it wasn't until she opened the door to the silent, fall air that she decided to walk to the car with him. She was seventeen years old at the time but not too young to make a deliberate and important alliance — an alliance which she knew would be denounced by her relatives, and which would be filled with both pain and joy for the rest of their lives.

11

Testimony: Day Two

October 1967

The second day of testimony opened as the chilly fall weather began in earnest. October. The earth was losing its summer warmth, and John's worries deepened. It wasn't just the cattle now. It was something else. It was a failure of values, a failure of community, a failure of esteem and respect among men, those ever-important considerations for Dakotahs.

This was the day that Jason Big Pipe began his testimony against John, and his appearance cut to the core of what was deepest and best in the view of the world that they both had learned throughout their lives. Many witnesses were subpoenaed, thus forced or manipulated into taking sides, but this one, John was told by his lawyer, volunteered. As it turned out, his testimony against his father's old friend initiated the public, familial, and tribal humiliation in the white man's court of law that John would forever afterward recall with a deep sense of loss.

Jason was now a man, no longer the infant that John had held on his knee, no longer the boy who had fished with him at the river's edge. Few people at the trial grasped the moral dimensions which now became the foremost considerations in the trial for John.

He does not believe that I have stolen my own cattle, thought John as he listened to the leading questions now being asked by the defense attorney, so that cannot be his motivation for slandering me. He doesn't, either, believe that I am incompetent, for he has worked side-by-side with me since he was old enough to saddle a horse. He rode with me as a youth, fixed fence, and put a brand on my cattle. This is a hostile act against me, and I know of no explanation for this young man's actions.

Justinian, the Roman lawyer and politician, who codified law in the context of Christianity, wrote in the sixth century that neither God nor human law could forbid all evil deeds, and if John Tatekeya had been a scholar of European history and religion, which he knew concentrated on the nature of evil, he might have agreed. But what he did know as a Dakotah was that the ethical aspect of "natural law," that to which a man is inclined naturally, the kind of law that the Dakotapi had always believed they specialized in, fails only when it is encouraged by reason and practicality and fate. There was no doubt that John considered this action of Jason's outside of the category of natural inclinations, and he would have to wait and see what explanations might emerge.

Joseph Nelson III began the questioning:

Q: Now, Jason Big Pipe, you are a young man of the tribe and you are knowledgeable about farming and ranching operations, would you say so?

A: Yeah.

Q: And you and your parents are neighbors of Mr. Tatekeya, is that so?

A: Yeah.

Q: Now, Mr. Big Pipe, you have identified the place which is Tatekeya's home place here on this map. (*pointing*) Will you show the jury where you say you saw his cattle out of his pasture? Where would they be?

A: This is the home place right here. (*indicating on a map*)

Q: Yes, now where would the cattle be out?

A: And this would be the highway. (*indicating again*)

Q: Yes?

A: It's got to be right in here (*indicating*), right through here. There's a fence line on this side of it. He should have put up better fences to hold them in.

Q: Now, this is all his pasture here. (*indicating*)

A: Yes. This is his whole unit here. (*indicating*)

Q: And where would they be, on the roads?

A: Yeah.

Q: How many would there be?

A: At that time about forty to fifty head. Maybe the whole bunch.

Q: Who would get those cattle back?

A: Well, he'd take a pickup out there and run them back in.

Q: Did he have any saddle horses on the place?

A: Yes, but he never used them.

Q: He didn't use them. Now, are you personally acquainted with Mr. Tatekeya's operation?

A: (*pause*) No.

Q: Well, what I mean is, you would see them, wouldn't you?

A: Yeah.

Q: What kind of a ranch manager was he?

A: Well, he ain't much of a manager. A lot of things he should have done better than what he's doing now.

Q: Has it improved recently?

A: No.

Q: Still as bad as ever?

A: Yeah.

Q: Now, do you know whether Mr. Tatekeya was ever absent, gone from his place?

A: Oh, yeah.

Q: Do you know how long a time he would be gone?

A: Yeah. There was a time there I think he was gone for a whole week.

Q: And when was that?

A: That year I don't remember. Well, let's see. That's in '64.

Q: '64. And how about in 1965?

A: Yeah, in '65, too.

Q: Was he there or gone in '65?

A: He was gone for about three, four days, or three days, maybe.

Q: When was that? Do you remember the time of year?

A: Well, in the summer some time.

Q: Now, did you ever run into Mr. Tatekeya anyplace off the ranch in 1965?

A: What was that?

Q: Did you ever find or see Mr. Tatekeya anyplace besides the ranch in 1965?

A: The place he'd go is to town, up north there.

Q: Were you there in Chamberlain in the fall of 1965?

A: Yes.

Q: Did you see Mr. Tatekeya?

A: Yeah. In the bar there.

Q: Do you know how long he was in Chamberlain?

A: Well, about a week; seven days or so.

Q: And where did you see him?

A: I seen him in the little Indian bar there in Chamberlain. They call it Buck's, I think.

Q: What was he doing when you saw him?

A: Well, he was under intoxication. He was drunk. I think he was still at it when I seen him; he was getting worse.

Q: How many occasions did you see him in that bar, how many times?

A: About four times. At least.

Q: And would those be on the same or separate days?

A: Separate days.

Q: I see. And on each of those occasions what was he doing?

A: Well, he was driving around in his pickup.

Q: And did you see him in the bar there, too?

A: Well, in the afternoon I seen him in the bar and towards evening he was in his pickup but he wasn't driving.

Q: Oh. He had somebody else driving?

A: Yes.

Q: Who was driving?

A: Some woman in there. I don't know.

Q: But, it was his pickup?

A: Oh, yeah . . . sure.

Q: Now, Mr. Big Pipe . . . you are . . .

12

John could feel the presence of his wife and daughter in the back of the room as Jason's words *Some woman in there. I don't know* reverberated and receded in the stuffy court-room. The unspeakable had been uttered and now it was out in the open and nothing would be the same. John looked out of the corner of his eye at the cowboy District Attorney who was making a big pretense of taking notes, his boots planted squarely in front of him. He stroked his eyebrow with his left thumb and forefinger, noncommittal, refusing to ac-knowledge John's tentative glance.

Just that morning, John's daughter had picked out the shirt he should wear to court.

"Wear this one, Ate," she had said with enthusiasm, hand-ing him a maroon and gray western-cut shirt she had helped him select in the store months ago. At breakfast with the family the eldest grandson had said, jokingly, "Lookin' go-o-oo-d, Grampa," fingering the sleeve of John's shirt and finally giving in to his emotions by flinging his arms about his grandfather and giving him a tremendous hug.

No, thought John now, sitting at the narrow table fearing the worst about what else Jason was going to say. But anything more could not hurt as much as this. Grampa doesn't look too good, *mitakoja*.

He was overcome momentarily by a sense of despair and deep sorrow for the shame these public proceedings would inflict upon his children, his wife, the young children who held him in high regard; upon Aurelia, whose only flaw was that she loved him; upon Benno and his father and all those who held on to the idea that what distinguished the Dakotapi from all others in this world was the powerful and compelling individual sense of obligation toward one's relatives.

Jason Big Pipe, the young man whose testimony was being used to discredit John Tatekeya, was the grandson of Red Shield, the old, respected leader of the Kaposia band of the Isianti, a contemporary of Benno's, a man who lived from crisis to crisis but one who provided for others' stability and faith in a world of swift and unpredictable transition.

When John was just a boy this old man had brought to the Tatekeya home the striped quills and the tobacco and requested that John's father take part in the important ceremony which would make them relatives, thus forever obliged to one another. John's father had participated in the ceremony because it was unheard of to refuse the invitation from a person of honor, even though his Christian wife had said that he must not do so.

"Be careful," she admonished him, "they will say that you are a heathen."

John's father had gone against his wife's wishes because he knew that the refusal to "make relatives" in the traditional way was to ultimately take part in the attempted destruction of the nationhood so relentlessly defended for hundreds of years by the people even before the invasion of their lands by Europeans.

John's father had been purified in the sweatlodge, and then he sat on the ground for the pipe ceremony. Benno had prepared the ground, brushing the leaves away from a small space and making four little holes filled with red and white plumes as the beginning of important vows.

Sitting before these, John's father had taken the sacred

pipe and held the pipestem to the ground saying, *"Uncheda, smoke this pipe and give me this day something to eat."*

The people in various groups had approached and entered the medicine lodge, and members of each group were made relatives to the other. To smoke ceremonially was to *wacekiya,* and what this meant, John's father had told him, was that these ancient rituals at Old Agency, done in secrecy because of the many levels of resistance and opposition by those in the community, these acts between the fathers and grandfathers renewed relationships and respect between them. These acts caused these relatives "to have trust in one another," he was told. *This is a sacred day. This is a sacred day. This is a sacred day. This is a sacred day.*

John looked at Jason's handsome face, his guileless eyes, and wondered what had prompted this young man's incriminating testimony against him. Why would this young man do this thing?

He knew no answer. And he began to believe that perhaps he deserved this kind of humiliation. He was himself, after all, culpable.

John looked out across the courtroom and saw Jason's older brother, Sheridan, sitting beside the huge, pale woman who was his wife. He looked like he was about to go to sleep, bored and sullen.

John glanced over at his own wife, her smooth face bland and expressionless. She was sitting beside their daughter in one of the back rows of the courtroom. Neither of them looked up at him.

After that public reference to "some woman in there" driving John's pickup, these two women so important in his life would cease attending the trial, and John knew he would not go to his daughter's home as the weekend recess loomed ahead. John also knew that they would not come again to the courthouse in support of him, and from that time he felt alone in the same way that he had felt alone since the death of Benno, and he wished for the whole insufferable, abusive ordeal to end. There will be no winners here, he thought.

13

Testimony: Day Two

(Continued)

Q: Now, Mr. Smith, where do you live?

A: Out in East Pierre.

Q: Are you a member of the tribe?

A: No sir. But I've always lived amongst 'em. Some of my best friends are them Indian boys out there.

Q: Now, during 1965, the months of January, first of all, we'll take it January to June of '65. Where were you living?

A: Now, let's see. I think I was living out on the reservation then. Yes, I was sort of camping out in an old house there that used to be the old Standing place. Just renting it, you know, for little or nothin' because I do some custom work out there now and then.

Q: Where is that from the home of Aurelia Blue?

A: Just across an eighty acres there.

Q: Across a pasture? Or a field?

A: Yes. I lived on the south side and she lived on the north side of that eighty.

Q: Did you know Mrs. Blue?

A: Yes. I know the young woman. And the old lady, too.

Q: Did you know Mr. Tatekeya's vehicle, what kind of a vehicle did he have then?

A: Yeah. He had an International pickup. I rode with him a few times.

Q: Did you ever see Mr. Tatekeya down there during that period of time?

A: Oh, yes! He was down there a lot. Well, I think he was down there practically ever' week. Sometimes . . . I don't know whether he was there, but when I'd go to bed his pickup was there, and when I'd get up in the morning it was there, and sometimes (*laughing*) it would be there 'til Wednesday, and sometimes Monday it would disappear. And, you know (*laughing*), you drawed your own conclusions. (*more seriously*) Generally, on Saturday is when it would show up, Saturday afternoon. (*nodding his head to show agreement with his own statement*)

Q: Have you ever been with Mr. Tatekeya in his home?

A: Yes. I was in that house twice just for a few minutes.

Q: When was that?

A: Oh, that was in . . . must have been the summer of '65.

Q: I see. On that occasion, did Mr. Tatekeya have occasion to tell his wife where he was going?

A: Yeah, well, he'd tell her that him and me was going to fix fences.

Q: Then where would he go?

A: Well, he'd generally wind up out to the Blue place. Sometimes I'd go with him, too.

Just as Mr. Smith began to warm to his subject, the judge intervened, saying, "Well, I think that all that's relevant here is the absence of Mr. Tatekeya from his place. I don't think we need to go into anything further, either the Aurelia Blue matter or anyplace else."

Looking at the District Attorney with just a trace of impatience, he said, "Sir. Mr. States Attorney. Mr. Cunningham. Do you have any objection?"

"Objection," Mr. Cunningham said, raising his voice finally. "Yes. I think that this is irrelevant."

"Well, now, your honor," said Mr. Nelson III, "may I go into the drinking patterns of Mr. Tatekeya, your honor?"

"You already have," said the judge. "You've certainly gone into that," he said, shaking his head. And then, "I have no objection. Certainly."

The questioning resumed:

Q: During this period, would you observe whether or not he was drinking?
A: Well, yes, we was both drinking a little. I drank a little myself at that time. I don't deny that. I haven't drank now for a year and a half, but at that time, I'll admit, I was drinking a little.
Q: And how much would Mr. Tatekeya drink?
A: Well, I don't know. It's hard to say. All he could get aholt of, I guess. (*laughing*) He done a fair job of drinking and a pretty fair job of holding it.
Q: Okay. That's all I have.

The District Attorney stood up and walked carefully to the middle ground. He cradled a pencil in the palm of his hand.

Q: Now, Mr. Smith. Are you a convicted felon?
A: What's . . . that?
Q: Are you a convicted felon?

"Objection, your honor," began the defense.
"Overruled," said the judge. "Answer the question, sir."

Q: Are you a convicted felon, Mr. Smith?
A: Well, but . . . that was . . .
Q: Answer the question, please.
A: Well, yes . . .
Q: No further questions.

14

That night, John and Aurelia lay quietly beside one another unable to put aside thoughts of the intimidating testimony of the past days.

"John," she said into the darkness. And, talking Indian, she mused, "When the grass dance was disclaimed by my mother and the people of her tribe, uh, well, you know . . . "

He said nothing.

The silence between them was taken over by their own private thoughts, which were filled with the flawless memories of a prophetic history they shared and both feared would end badly. Only now were they beginning to understand that events would move relentlessly forward, that there was little they could do.

When they had both nearly forgotten her half-finished sentence, John answered, "Yes. I know." And he covered his eyes with his arm, pretending to be unmoved by this intimate feeling that Aurelia was trying to express.

She continued, then.

"They said, I mean, the Christians said and therefore some of the people said, too, that to take off their clothes and paint themselves was evil and they should not dance to those precious songs."

He listened in silence to this story of hers, not really attentive to the subject matter because he had heard her tell it many times, and he knew that his mother, too, had been a part of this startling, shameless truth of history, and so the story itself was nothing new.

Aurelia went on.

"They said to pray to the east, west, north, and south" — in the darkness he could feel her motioning with her hands — "was to pray to the winds, and it was, therefore, evil."

With her slim fingers she lifted her heavy, black hair from her neck and smoothed it behind her ear, and he felt her move toward him.

"And my mother came to believe that." She drew herself up as though feeling suddenly cold.

"M-m-m."

He turned toward her and touched the warmth between her bare thighs, and in the darkness, he could feel her look at him as if from far away, smiling.

"A-aye-e-e," she scoffed quietly, pushing his hand away. "You're always *doing* that."

But she turned to him quickly, stretched full-length beside him, and her body was warm and soft, and the story she was telling him, as she had told it before, was forgotten. For the moment. John felt the tension in his body diminish as she held him.

Aurelia fell asleep in his arms, and as she slept, he struggled with his thoughts. Jason's testimony. How the testimony of the old drunk, Smitty, made him look like a fool, and, ultimately, what the woman beside him thought of her own intimate participation in such a debacle. Even more puzzling, what was it that the woman beside him wanted from him as she tried to fathom the impact of the aggressive religion and law of white men upon the people and their lives?

He could not help her. There will be no reprieve, he thought. No means of escape. At that moment, in the darkness, John instinctively knew and, regretfully, accepted the fact that it was over. The solemn and extraordinary liaison that he and Aurelia treasured would, finally, be done. Forever changed. His desire reconciled. And her urgency turned to indifference.

How Aurelia felt about her mother's response to new religious thought and practice had begun to take on a kind of desperate importance for her, and John feared that it would, sooner or later, be clear to her that she, too, like her mother, and his, had played with marked cards, played her hand against her will. The game would have to be taken into account. By all of us, thought John.

Because he was the only one who knew of her fragmented but continuous attempts at understanding her mother's rejection of tradition, John began to wonder in recent months, and especially since the trial began, if she was going to be able to reconcile herself to the consequence of this trial, their separation.

He again felt the anxiety about the outcome of the trial. Not whether he would win or lose. Not whether he would get paid for his missing cattle or have them returned to him. Not even whether the thief would be punished or go free. Rather, his fear that an honorable life for his people was no longer possible rose in his throat. There were so many things that he had not paid attention to, and he knew now what terrible risk there was in such inattentiveness.

It was true that the young man who had stolen his cattle, a young white man who had grown up on his parents' ranch bordering the reservation, the spoiled son of well-to-do white cattlemen and -women, was no bargain as far as the white community which surrounded John's place was concerned, and it might be true, too, that Smitty's damaging testimony gave people a bad impression of John. But it was only when he heard it aloud, spoken in the courtroom, it was only then, when he looked into the eyes of the people who loved him, that John acknowledged in his heart the uncompromising pride and courage inherent in the Dakotah way of life, and the loss of it, momentarily at least, in the behavior of everyone connected with this miserable trial. Now, at this trial, humiliated in front of his loved ones, he knew that the claims the Dakotahs had always made concerning their ideals would never again be seen as invincible. Not by him. Not by those who were present at this gathering. That was the price of the entrenchment of white civilization in his life and the lives of others.

Jason Big Pipe's testimony rang in his ears, and he knew that for some the old, familial bonds of respect for one another, those significant communal codes of behavior as old as the tribes themselves, were no longer held as intrinsically valuable. It began long ago, he now believed. But because of the recent flooding of the homelands, the constant moving about and resettlement, and the repeated destruction of the places where the people were born and buried for century upon century, one generation upon the next generation, it was now a crucial matter.

He sat up, naked and shivering.

Who would his children be?

Where would his children live? His grandchildren?

In the darkness, he buried his head in his hands. It was these kinds of questions that kept John awake at Aurelia's side that night. For his deep-seated suspicion would not go away: the attempt to find justice in the white man's law would unwittingly reveal the fraudulent nature of all their lives and the lives of those who were to come after him.

15

Testimony: Day Three

October 1967

Nothing could have prepared those at the trial for the subtle meaning of the events of the third day of testimony, and indeed, for many of them, the testimony held little significance beyond the rather generalized setting forth of the so-called material facts in the case. For John Tatekeya, however, the time had come to put his suspicions to the test. As he took the witness stand again, he had determined in some forlorn yet angry way, deciding on the spur of the moment in just the few minutes that it took him to walk from his vehicle into the courthouse, that he would sift purpose from this otherwise empty and insignificant ritual in whatever way he could.

He lingered briefly on the steps of the gray, imposing building and pulled the smoke heavily from his cigarette, inhaling deeply. Such a day as this, he thought, held no promise at all, unless one forced out the existent decay which it held with whatever distasteful and foul means were at hand. Goddamn! Son-of-a-bitch!

With his third finger and thumb, he flicked his cigarette butt viciously toward the gutter and entered the building through the heavy glass doors, passing the dignified, bearded sentinel without a glance.

Q: Now, Mr. Tatekeya, since the fall of 1965, have you seen any of those missing cattle since then?
A: Yes. I seen several of them.
Q: You have?
A: Yes.
Q: Where did you see them?
A: Well, I seen one of them over there north of Highmore. I seen one of them up east of Yankton, by Irene.
Q: And did you see one down there, near Ainsworth, Nebraska?
A: I seen *a couple of them* down there.

At this answer, unexpected but hoped for by the young white man's defense attorney, John looked squarely into the cowboy's disbelieving and astonished eyes, then at Mr. Joseph Nelson III, who saw his chance and leapt to his feet shouting triumphantly, "Just a moment! Your honor!"

Waving his arm at the judge, he called, "I have a motion. I have a motion."

Because of a technicality, the second critter at Ainsworth which John identified in testimony was not mentioned in the indictment, and those closely connected with the trial knew that his seemingly offhand mention of "a couple of them" was a blow to his case. Three critters were named in the indictment. Not four. A cause for mistrial, surely.

"May we approach the bench?" asked the District Attorney, agitated, fearful.

"You may," answered the judge.

As the three lawyers conferred quietly but earnestly, John looked over at Sheridan's heavy, round face. He was no longer lounging carelessly in his seat. The young man's eyes were suddenly alert, attentive, and he leaned over to whisper something to his wife, who looked merely frightened. He grabbed his brother Jason's knee and then hit it with his fist lightly, triumphantly.

John stared into Sheridan's face and knew, at that moment, that he had put together some of the pieces of the puzzle. The missing information. He knew now why Harvey had been so noncommittal when he had gone to his place to ask for help in finding his cattle. He knew now why the Big Pipe brothers had attended this trial so fastidiously and why Sheridan lounged in the spectators' seats so casually every day, though he was neither witness nor participant. And he knew now why Jason Big Pipe, the relative of his grandfather Red Shield and the middle son of his own brother, had testified falsely against him.

The sons of Harvey Big Pipe, John decided at that moment, had been engaged in the theft more fully than they had let on, quite possibly as participants in the actual crime. Gravely, seriously, John took in these thoughts and began to realize that if he never knew anything further concerning the theft, and even if he lost the trial, which was quite possible now, he would not again feel pain with such temporal clarity. He sat still, astounded. Humbled. His face felt feverish. The blood throbbed in his temples.

Judge Niklos excused the jury, and the twelve men who were sitting in judgment on this strange little drama began to file out of the courtroom into their small chambers. Some of them, who had seen nothing significant in the testimony and had perhaps not heard the Tatekeya statement, looked around the room, confused and perplexed.

"I will see the defendant and his lawyer in my office," the judge said, looking at John.

"But first, Mr. Nelson, what do you have to say?"

"Comes, now, the defendant and moves for a mistrial," said Mr. Nelson III with enthusiasm, "upon the grounds and for the reason that shortly before the commencement of this trial, a motion was made for a continuance on the grounds that a fourth cow had not been disclosed to the defendant and his attorney, in accordance with the pretrial order of the court and the discovery proceedings, at this time the United States Attorney agreed that no mention would be made of the fourth critter. No pictures were introduced. And that he would caution his witnesses not to mention the fourth animal in Nebraska."

He drew in his breath and read on from notes obviously prepared beforehand for just such an eventuality as this. The defense, it seemed, had been lying in wait for such an answer and could not contain its glee.

He read on:

"That the court indicated that in light of that ruling or that announcement by the United States Attorney, the motion for continuance would be denied.

"That the fourth animal has now been mentioned by the complaining witness before this jury. The jury heard the testimony and, by necessity, it was brought home more to them because of this motion.

"That this is prejudicial; it violates the rights of the defendant in this matter, in that the continuance was not granted.

"That the fact that it was unintentional, if such is the fact, does not any the less remove the prejudice of the defendant's rights. The jury now knows of a fourth cow."

In his chambers, the judge turned to the District Attorney.

"What do you have to say, Mr. Cunningham?"

Visibly shaken, the cowboy lawyer looked over at his client.

"Mr. Tatekeya," he began uncertainly and slowly. "Do you remember my talking to you in my rooms about not mentioning that steer calf down there in Ainsworth?"

"Yes."

"I take it that it was . . ." He groped for words and started again.

Clearing his throat, "I take it that it was . . . just an accident? Had you forgotten about that when you mentioned that you found two of them down there?"

"It could be. I'm not an expert in this courtroom . . . so . . ." John, spreading his hands on his knees, refused to look at his lawyer.

"Well, your honor," the District Attorney said, turning to the judge, "I'm sure that the witness did it unintentionally.

The court and counsel is well aware of the fact that the witness is not one of a very high education."

John still did not look up.

The lawyer went on, "He's been, you know, a rather difficult witness to handle as far as the questioning is concerned, and I'm certain that whatever he did or said, it was not intentional.

"Furthermore," he said, gathering his composure, "I'm certain that no prejudice was created by any such comment by the witness before the jury; in fact, I . . . uh . . . I think that the statement was probably not even heard by many of the jurors. It wasn't said very loudly. And I certainly didn't intend to have the witness disclose two head of cattle down there at Ainsworth, even though we took pictures of both for evidence and, I think, it's obvious from the way I asked the question. I think of any question I asked, that was certainly a leading question."

The conference in the judge's chambers became more composed as the District Attorney talked in a reasonable tone and the judge attempted to regain the protocol expected of this proceeding.

"Sir," the judge said, addressing Mr. Cunningham, "I assume from the question that you asked Mr. Tatekeya, you did assure him that he was to strictly limit his testimony to three cows, or three animals at least, and not to mention the fourth."

"That's correct, your honor," the District Attorney responded. "But, after all, he *is* missing forty-two head, and he doesn't like the idea that we're going to trial on only three. And that this technicality should . . ."

"Now, now . . . ," admonished the judge, in a tone something like that of an all-knowing adult addressing a recalcitrant child. "You know as well as I do that is immaterial to this particular indictment. This indictment, let me remind you, is for three animals and three animals only. You surely know the law, and the only question now is, does your client know the law?"

With that, he turned to John.

"Now, Mr. Tatekeya, how much education have you had?"

John said nothing.

Mr. Niklos began again, enunciating carefully, thinking that John did not understand the question.

"How far did you go in school?"

"Oh, about far enough . . . ," John said tiredly.

Sternly, the judge said, "Just a minute now, Mr. Tatekeya. You must answer my question. How much education have you had?"

"I passed the sixth grade at Rapid City Indian School," John answered, paused, and then volunteered, "and then I went into the army. It was 1916."

He thought it best not to mention that he had lied about his age to get into the U.S. Army, that he was not even a citizen of the United States at the time, that he had run away from that boarding school like an escapee from a jail, and that his educational experience had been limited, mostly, to learning to speak English, play the clarinet, and milk cows.

"Well," said the judge rather vacantly, not realizing that this educational and military experience was probably on a par with or even superior to most of the educational experience of the white farmers and ranchers in the area, and therefore not evidence that John was in any way incapacitated.

"Very well." Absently.

"I'll tell you. I'm tempted," he said to the room at large. "I'd just as soon go home, actually. I'd like to grant the motion for a mistrial."

Do it, thought John.

"Your honor," began Mr. Nelson III, trying to take advantage of this seeming pause and hesitation on the part of the judge. "I would like to say this: the fact that the U.S. Attorney might have cautioned him does not remove the prejudice and the error."

"Well, Mr. Nelson. I'm going to tell you this: I am not certain that the jury heard the remark, either. It was said in a rather low manner. I know the court reporter heard it. And I heard it."

"And I heard it, your honor," said Nelson.

"And you heard it," repeated the judge, smiling. "And you were looking for it, weren't you? I don't think there is any question about that! And I'm not sure whether the jury heard it or not."

The room fell silent momentarily, and the only sound John could hear was the ticking of the huge clock which stood at the end of the room. The prospect of finishing the trial filled John with despair, for it seemed obvious to him now that this judge and these lawyers could do nothing for him. He listened with little interest as they resolved the dilemma his testimony had presented.

"Now," the judge told Mr. Nelson, "if you want me to, I will caution the jury and tell them, right now, when I have them come back in, that they are to consider only three cows, that there are only three cows in question in this indictment; that he's testified here already that he missed a lot of other calves and yearlings but that they are to consider the testimony only as it relates to three critters and that all the other cows are not to be considered. Nor are they to draw any possible inference that this defendant had anything to do . . . and that he's not even charged with any more than three cows."

The judge dabbed at his face with a white monogrammed handkerchief and sat cleaning his glasses.

"Now, if you want me to so instruct the jury, I'll do it at this time."

He paused and put his glasses on, looking up at the defense attorney, and folded his handkerchief carefully, lifting up the folds of his black gown and putting the handkerchief in his shirt pocket.

"Now, if you prefer I not so instruct the jury, I won't. But I'm leaving it up to you."

"I feel, your honor," said Joseph Nelson III, a young man whose father and grandfather had both, in the not-so-distant past, tried cases before this same judge, and who saw himself as therefore having a family reputation which he thought would get him a more favorable ruling, "I feel, your honor, that such an instruction would work to the prejudice of my client, the defendant."

"Very well, then," said Judge Niklos. "I will not so instruct the jury."

"But," protested young Nelson, "that my client, in light of this, is entitled to a mistrial."

"Well," said the judge, "I'm going to deny your motion for a mistrial."

As he got up from his desk, he said cheerily to all, "Now, do you want a little recess?"

16

Inexplicably, a three-day recess in the trial was called by the judge, a move which was seen by John as just another delay and an unreasonable way to prolong his own personal agony. He was looking for any excuse now to quit this matter.

As John and the District Attorney walked back into the courtroom to collect their belongings and leave the building, the lawyer said tightly, "That was a close one, John."

"This thing could have gone into a mistrial over that mistake, John," he said, "and we can't afford another one like that! But, I think we're okay. Remember, John, you can't . . . "

As the lawyer paused, trying to find the right words to chastise his client, John said quietly, "I have a good memory, cowboy."

"Uh . . ."

They looked at each other warily.

Instead of leaving the building, they both sat down suddenly at one of the tables and started to talk and listen to one another for the first time since the case had come to trial.

"I cannot begin to explain what happened as I answered your questions, lawman," said John, "because it is of no concern to you and it is too complicated. But one thing you must understand from me is that all of us who were born in this country naked have been taught something other than your ways. What you talk about and what you care about has very little to do with my life. Do you understand that?"

"No, of course I don't," said the lawyer.

"And besides," he went on indignantly, "I just don't believe it. The law is important to everyone's life, John, even an Indian's. Maybe *especially* an Indian's."

"Mr. Cunningham, we have been taught from the time we are infants that with all of the people around us we should live happy and friendly with them and then we will have everything turn out all right," John said. "Everything in our way of life points to the idea of doing the right things with our relatives. Your history books say that all the Dakotahs and Lakotahs do is fight and murder all the time. That is not true about us, you know. We know how to live with our relatives."

This was the longest speech that John had engaged in since the attorney had met him, and the white man tried to make sense of what he was saying.

John knew that he was not getting across what was most significant on his mind, and he ruefully thought about Jason and Sheridan, the sons of his own brother who had somehow and for some reason violated the ways that the people had worked out for thousands of years as survival tactics in a hostile and dangerous world. John did not know how to explain the significance of this finding to his lawyer.

He got up and walked across the room. He pulled a pack of cigarettes from his shirt pocket and offered one to his lawyer, who shook his head and said only, "Those things are bad for you, John."

John carefully lit one for himself, drawing the smoke deep into his lungs.

"You know, lawman, this circus here" — he waved his arm to indicate the courtroom still being cleared for the recess — "it is all being done to shame me, to make me look bad."

"Well, John . . . ," began the District Attorney, who then lapsed into silence, sensing that his lecture on unbounded pride might not be useful at this moment.

Quietly, John continued: "I do not agree to this foolishness! And I do not want to go on with it."

He looked deeply into the lawyer's eyes, trying to convince him that terrible damage had been done as the result of this trial and it would be forever seen as a threat to the faith and humanity of his relatives. But he said only, "This young white man who stole forty-two head of my cattle, he can sit there and lie and pretend his innocence and he does not even have to testify. He will not come to the stand as I have done."

He paused.

"The lawyers ask me questions about things that are none of their business and suggest that I stole my own cattle. How do you account for such a stupid way of getting to the truth of things? What is this?" he asked indignantly.

"I do not agree to this foolishness," he repeated with more vigor this time, jamming his cigarette into the ashtray.

Instantly, the lawyer knew that he must prevent John from walking away from this.

"But you will agree, John," he argued, "if you expect this man to be convicted on this indictment and if you expect to get justice. You did agree essentially when you came to this trial."

"Do not misunderstand me, lawyer," John said tersely, angry now and thinking seriously about walking out of the courtroom, out of the building, and driving back to his place on the reservation.

"I am an Indian, just like that judge said," explained John. "And what that means these days is that I've got myself to look after. I don't have anything invested in your law, and it has never defended me or my people. I don't have my forty-two head of cattle. I don't have any reason to believe that I will be paid for them even if we win this case. The most I could get is payment for three head."

John sat at the edge of his chair with his head down, his elbows resting on his knees.

"I am a poor man, you know, and I am mad as hell that I have been made even poorer now," he said.

He could talk about these things that made him angry during this unexpected moment of intimacy between himself and the attorney for the United States of America, but what he would not talk about was the thing which brought him the greatest sorrow: the unaccountable behavior of two young men, the Big Pipe brothers for whom he had been supportive as they had grown to adulthood, two young men whose parents had accepted eagle plumes from John after each birth.

Aloud he said, "I don't have my reputation. You can see here that many people have testified against me. Yet I am not the thief! Even my wife refuses to come and listen to this with my eldest daughter. I don't have the goodwill and respect of anyone here. Not even you, lawman, if you were to be honest."

He had seen the shame in the lawyer's manner when Jason Big Pipe had talked of the woman driving his rig, intimating that John might be involved in what the lawyer would surely term adulterous behavior.

The lawyer said nothing.

"I have only the pity of some people. They're saying 'that poor goddamned son-of-a-bitch.' And the hatred of others."

The sullen face of Sheridan Big Pipe flashed before him, and the testimony of Jason echoed in the marble halls of the courthouse. What has happened here? John tried to understand the hatred of these young men toward him. The extent to which present behavior may be accounted for in terms of historical expectations troubled John, and he fell to thinking about the issues of this kind raised in his recent conversations with Aurelia. What happens to the people when new ways are forced upon us? Do we begin to hate one another? If so, why? When my mother became a Christian, did she set in motion my uncertainty? As my land is inundated by the white man's deliberate flood, is my spirit also weeping for its lost strength? Is Benno looking for me? What can I do now?

Such questions were profoundly disturbing.

"Listen, John," said the lawyer, suddenly drawing John's attention back to the stuffy courtroom. "You can feel sorry for yourself if you want to, but I'm not going to let you give up. I'm going to win this case for you because it is right and fair for us to win. No one hates you here, John," he said as he picked up his briefcase.

John stood with his back to his lawyer, gazing out of the window at the street below. Noon traffic clogged the four-way stop, and people straggled from the Federal Building into the restaurants and shops across the street. An old man with a cane made his way slowly down a side street, away from the people and the traffic, and John found himself wondering where the old man was headed. And as he stood in deep thought, he knew more than ever now that winning or losing the trial did not matter.

Silence hung in the warm, close air.

The lawyer tried again. "John, you can't afford to have all this pride. Don't worry about your reputation. So what if some things have come out that make you look bad? What we need to do is . . ." And then he changed his thoughts: "John, have you heard that to have too much pride is to . . ."

"Yes. I have heard that," said John, interrupting. "Christians say pride goeth before a fall. I am not totally without knowledge, you see," John said as he turned and smiled for the first time since the conversation began.

"It comes from the Bible, yes? A story about Adam and Eve, first man and first woman, something like the *Tokahe*, I suppose. They were told to leave the Garden because they disobeyed God, is that so?"

"Yes."

"So, what do you think it means?" asked John.

"What it means," said the lawyer with certainty, "is that arrogance in the face of justice and the law and God is no virtue, John. Do you know what I am getting at?"

John lapsed into silence.

"Do you know what arrogance really means, John?" asked the cowboy lawyer tentatively.

In near despair now, John looked at his lawyer and forced a smile. You and I will never understand each other, he thought. How can you chastise me, a Dakotah, about arrogance when it has been your people who have forced your religion on everyone throughout the world, your people who changed the rivers that we live by and flooded our lands and brought to us the kind of world that Gray Plume and Benno and the others feared?

John picked up his jacket and turned with seriousness to his lawyer. As he shook hands with him, he said, "I am grateful to you for your efforts here in this courtroom. I know that you are a sincere man."

He walked out the door.

The lawyer looked after him wondering if he had insulted him. He worried that his client might not show up for the Tuesday morning session.

John had said nothing to the lawyer about what he had finally begun to accept concerning the significance of this trial, for it had precious little to do with arrogance and justice and God. It was the understanding which came to him while he watched Sheridan's face during the testimony that morning. I put the case up for grabs, so to speak, thought John, and when I did so Sheridan behaved in such a way that I knew he had more than just a passing interest in its outcome. While this issue may have seemed to the District Attorney, had he known about it, parochial and trivial, it consumed the thoughts of Tatekeya.

It is not only that I now know Harvey Big Pipe's sons to be implicated in the theft, he mused. I know too that their father, the man with whom I am expected to behave as a brother, the man with whom I share important responsibilities, this man and I share the risk of losing our lives as brothers for the first time in nearly half a century.

Frail and sick, unable to work and take active part in community affairs, Harvey would now be faced with loss of the sacred meaning of trust in his brother, a relationship which signified for them both the moral quality of the social world in which their kinship duties were strictly ordered.

As he drove toward his daughter's house located out on Airport Road, John suddenly made a left turn at the stoplight and headed east toward the reservation. Traces of snow fell on his windshield, the merest flecks of icy moisture which melted as quickly as they touched the glass.

Part Two

Summation

A Recapitulation

The Man That Is Struck by the Ree

"I am not going to beg for my life; I believe I am a man, and I am not going to beg you for my life. I see you here, and your manners and situation are enough to scare any of us; but if I was afraid I would squat down, but I don't."
(Translation)

Summer 1856

17

At home, alone, John stood at the door peering into the dusk at the sparse snowflakes drifting down, minute light flakes which probably wouldn't last long, the kind recognized by those who live on the Dakota prairie as fleeting signs, brief warnings of the beginning of winter, harbingers of those freezing, blinding blizzard winds which often accompany the relentless cold.

The wet flakes melted listlessly away. To John they seemed gentle, almost benign, though he knew better. With a fork, he speared chunks of the boiled beef from the cold broth left setting out in a bowl on the kitchen table, careful to remember not to use any salt. He ate them hungrily, gulped down the rest of his coffee, and pulled on his leather gloves.

It would be dark in a couple of hours, he thought. Even now, the sky, the dull glare of the river, and the whitened, cold earth merged into a bluish-white grayness that chilled him to the bone. This would be only the first of several brief cold snaps that would precede the relentless winter, and he looked forward to the inevitable letup which invariably followed these first signs, thinking about tomorrow when it would probably turn warm, and the sun would shine, and he could fix fence in his shirtsleeves.

He dreaded the two-mile walk to the church and he was tempted to drive, but he decided to follow Benno's wishes again this time.

"You should always walk," Benno used to tell him. "Because then you have time to think and prepare yourself, and whatever is around you can tell you what you need to know.

"It is a good time, then," Benno said, "to get yourself ready."

But now he was in a hurry and he was late. He had to open up the building and get his own things ready. The little water drum, the hide, along with the seven stones, were kept in his bedroom, and he had to make sure that he delivered them to his nephew, who tied the drum, in time to ready it for the ritual singing and drumming.

This would probably be the last service to be held in the little church before the bad winter weather set in, after which they would meet in the members' homes. Ordinarily, John would be perspiring in his preparations, and he would have to take off the extra sweater he wore, but this time, for some inexplicable reason, he felt a chill.

People would probably bring blankets to cover their legs or shoulders throughout the night, he thought. And then, selfishly, he wondered how much they knew about his trial. News travels fast in this community, he thought, and one might say that bad news travels especially fast. He smiled and decided that it didn't matter.

When he walked into the barren churchyard, several cars were already there, motors running. But he paid no attention to the fact that he was late again. He noticed Harvey's daughter Clarissa sitting in her car, waiting, with her two boys and her mother. Harvey wasn't with them.

John hurried into the building, opening the unlocked door, and hauled some wood and kindling into the back room. He lighted a small fire in the black, oblong heating stove. Harvey's grandson Philip helped him, dashing in and out with armsful of wood and offering a match when John searched futilely in his pockets. Outside near the sweat-lodge, which was almost hidden in the brush, the fire man already stirred the glowing embers in preparation for the sacred fire which would be placed in a crucible in the middle of the room, to be replenished and reshaped throughout the night.

"Is your grampa sick?"

"Yeah."

"Why didn't he come? Gray Iron will be here, and maybe he could help him."

"I don't know."

People began drifting in and seating themselves around the room wherever they could be comfortable. Some of the older women brought pillows and blankets with them; the younger people with children brought sacks of extra clothes, bedding for infants, were settling the children and spreading blankets.

John felt helpless as he watched the young man beside him, for he was reminded of himself so many years ago. He had been content to work as an assistant to Benno, to learn the songs, a helper to his father and others for whom the philosophical speculation concerning the meaning of life was a serious matter. And he could see that this young man was also one with great potential such as he had possessed at one time. He knew that it had been widely expected that he would, sooner or later, enter into these religious matters as a significant figure, but, of course, he had not done so. He was a devotee and a believer in the medicine. He knew all the songs. And he continued to help in whatever way he could. But nothing more was possible for him.

Often he served as instructor to the young children who gathered at these festivities, especially those meetings held in the summer.

"Your own tipi will have four sacred poles," he would tell the younger relatives.

"You must have the three main poles" — and he would cross the forefinger of his right hand over two fingers of his left hand — "and, then, one which is the doorpost."

He would turn his right hand over and then lay two fingers diagonally across the others.

He repeated his grandmother's story, that these poles "represented the land tortoise because of all the animals, that land tortoise had the strongest paws, and as a consequence, it was adapted to hold up the lodge."

"Besides," she told him, "he is the mythological creature who makes the apposition between the water and the land a bridge and not an abyss."

John returned to the stove and stood there with Philip, warming his hands and waiting for the singers to compose themselves. He wanted to speak to the young man, tell him all the stories he knew about the preparations for such religious ceremonies.

"I haven't told those stories in a very long time," he said aloud to the young man and then said nothing more, leaving Philip puzzled and quiet. The thought occurred to John that he was very likely no longer worthy for such tellings, for when the fathers and Benno had approached the medicine lodge and sent out invitations over and over again, they sorrowed silently that John was never among the real initiates.

It was a sad thing for Benno, who had many expectations of his children, and it was with regret that John recognized that he had been, indeed, a disappointment to others. The way he lived his life and conducted himself certainly lacked propriety, and no one was more aware of it than John himself.

He looked at the young man standing in front of him. And he said nothing.

Later, as the drum chief knelt beside him, he sang: "*Heciya ya yo wiconi ye ye do. Heciya ya yo wiconi ye ye do. Heciya ya yo wiconi ye ye do. Cekiya ya yo wiconi ye ye do heyana he de do we.*" He began to feel warm. Soon he would have to remove his coat and sweater. And the spirits would surely come.

18

He was more tired than he cared to own up to, but he consoled himself as he walked home the next morning by remembering that Benno would have found such a day as this one calming, soothing, and he would make the most of it. The sun rose higher in the sky, the leaves were golden and withered, and the air was sharp and sweet. The glare of the river blinded him and he turned away. It's that time of year, he thought, when you just want to fold your arms and sit in the warm sun.

Instead, when he reached his place he swung the tailgate of his rig open and carefully placed spools of barbed wire, sacks of nails and a hammer, his posthole auger, and a wire stretcher in the long narrow bed. He motioned for the dog to jump in and sit.

He drove down the graveled road about two miles, pulled off into the ditch, then up to the fence lines, and parked. He began the tedious task of stretching the fifth barbed wire on that half-mile hillside next to the watering trough where the cattle always seemed to sense the weakness of only four wires.

With the sun climbing into the sky behind him warming

his back, he thought about his dilemma and wondered what his mother, that lady of propriety and manners and modesty, the daughter of a respected Isianti Presbyterian churchman from Old Agency, would think of this impeachment which had suddenly become a part of his life, though he had neither sought it nor given it purpose. He held each end of the short rod and walked backward laying down the wire on the ground diagonally to the posts. Absorbed, he began tacking the wire to the fence posts.

He didn't hear his younger brother drive up and was startled by his voice.

"Hey, they got you workin', huh?" Dan hollered from the window of his red Pontiac four-door.

John looked up and smiled.

"Where the hell you been?" he asked.

He walked over to the passenger's side, opened the door, and sat down beside his brother.

They shook hands and John repeated his question.

"It's not where I been," said Dan, laughing. "It's where I'm going."

He reached under the seat, took out a bottle of Early Times, unscrewed the cap, and took a long drink.

Smiling, he handed the bottle to John, who shook his head.

"All right," John said, trying to enter into the good mood, "where you going?"

And they both laughed.

Relaxed now, they sat together and looked out over the brown hills. John lit up a cigarette, cupping the match with his hands. The wind was gusting a bit now, and the dried leaves and grasses rolled gently. Stark white clouds hung against the brilliant blue of the sky, and a small cluster of birds swung toward the river.

Neither of them mentioned the trial.

"I'm headed to Bismarck for the celebration," said Dan, breaking the brief silence between them. "You want to come along?" His words drifted into the insistent wind.

"I'm broke," said John.

"Hell, what else is new?" scoffed his brother. "You won't have no coins tomorrow either, will you? Or the next day? Or next week?"

He pulled out his wallet and showed John several hundred-dollar bills and gave him one.

"Hey," he said enthusiastically, "I sold that Appie mare that Steven has been wanting and I made him pay for her. Look at that," and he slapped his hand against the wallet.

"You coming?"

"Yeah," said John. "Just a minute."

He walked back to the fence, cut the wire at the last post, placed the spool of wire in the cab of his pickup along with the rest of his tools, locked both doors to the rig, and left it parked alongside the fence.

"Let's go," he said as he got in Dan's car and slammed the door.

The dog, accustomed to such inconsistencies, turned down the opposite way and headed for home, trotting amiably, listing to one side, tongue lapping.

John and his youngest brother had not seen each other in several months, and as they settled in for the long drive to Bismarck they began to catch up on their lives. Dan put the bottle of whiskey under the seat and began to reminisce.

"You remember that time we sold them chickens, John?" he said, laughing.

"Jeez," he went on, "that was a long time ago, ennit?"

John's three little girls had come running toward Dan as he entered the house.

He picked them all up, tussled one onto his back and held the other two, one in each arm.

"What did you bring us, Uncle Dan?"

"Say, I didn't bring you nothin' this time," he said seriously as he bent over and put them all down on the floor. "I forgot."

He could see by their faces that they didn't believe him, so he pulled three Tootsie Rolls from his pocket and gravely handed them out, one for each little girl, the youngest getting hers first, then the middle child, then the eldest. They shook hands with him politely.

"Ina is in the hospital," they told him. "We don't know when she will come back."

Dan went into the kitchen and spoke to the woman he called his mother, the sister of his deceased blood mother, the woman who had raised him since childhood.

"He's out in the barn," she told him and then turned her back when she smelled the liquor on his breath, indicating that she was not interested in any further conversation with him.

John was putting the horse tack away when Dan approached him and asked if he wanted to go to Bismarck.

The dialogue was strangely precursory:

"I got no coins, younger brother, my wife's in the hospital at the Fort, and things are pretty tough around here."

"Yeah," Dan said, lurching just a little as he put one foot up on a railing. "But I got this," as he pulled a bottle from under his jacket.

"We sat there for nearly an hour," John remembered. "We got damn drunk, you know it? And that's when we got the idea."

Liberated by the booze to begin what he then considered to be a creative idea, John had said, "Listen, when the chickens go to roost, let's catch a bunch of them and stuff them in these empty grain bags. We can take them over to old Rasmussen. He'll buy them from us."

"Good idea," Dan had agreed.

The sun was just beginning to dip behind the hills when John and Dan got out some long wires from the hay barn, bent them into deep hooks at one end, and crept toward the chicken house "like a couple of wet dogs looking for a place to shake," they'd said later. They waited. Then they opened the door stealthily and stood in the darkness listening attentively to the muffled clucking of one or two of the more suspicious old birds.

The first two catches were executed brilliantly, and it wasn't until the chickens began squawking as they were stuffed into the grain bags that the whole operation went awry.

Alerted by their more unfortunate sisters, the roosting hens began to step agilely out of the way of the wire hooks. Some began to screech loudly and flap their wings, flying blindly like untargeted missiles toward the brothers' heads. John's hat was knocked off and he felt it crunch under his boot as he lurched forward, off-balance, then caught himself. Like a player in some kind of relentless farce, Dan fell toward the roosts, breaking one long pole from its moorings and whacking John across the nose with it as it swung toward the door.

The air was filled with chicken feathers. The loud squawking stirred the dogs from their sleeping places under the porch and brought them yelping toward the little chicken house. They scratched on the closed door and barked frantically. They started digging in the dirt at the door.

"I pressed myself against the wall and just stood there," John remembered. He had touched his nose carefully with one gloved hand and poked gently at the soft tissue under his eye, knowing full well that he'd have to explain his black eye to everybody for the next several days.

"You were cussin'!" he said, laughing.

As if by some prearranged signal, they had both tried to stand quietly, scarcely breathing. John heard Dan thrashing around and swearing softly in the midst of the feathers. He knew that the woman who was his mother must be standing at the door of the house listening to all this, but he also knew that she wouldn't interfere. At last, though, all got quiet for a minute and the hens went back to their roosting places. The dogs returned to their beds under the porch.

"Hey," John whispered loudly. "You OK?"

"Yeah."

"You want to quit?"

"Hell, no. I'm not quittin'. I just . . . got . . . to be . . . a little more careful."

Dan then pulled himself up from a crouching position. He decided that he would crawl under the tiered roosts and quietly pick off the hens from behind with his bare hands. John heard him crawling slowly under the roosts.

They both waited, again, for the hens to settle down.

John hooked a bird neatly, this time quickly grabbing her wings so that she couldn't flap them, and he stuffed her into the bag.

In the quiet he heard Dan swear hoarsely, "Jee-e-e-sus Christ!"

"Taku? Taku?"

"That goddamned chicken shit went down my neck!"

John guffawed.

And, later, "Jee-e-e-sus Christ!" Dan repeated. "The stink on these goddamned chickens . . . whoo-o-o-e-e-e-e."

But he, too, was hurriedly stuffing the birds in his sack, oblivious to the ludicrous spectacle of two grown men crouching in this smelly, cramped chicken coop making off with some of the most unattractive of God's creatures.

"Shit!" Dan muttered redundantly. "I never did like chickens." And then, "Jee-sus, they smell, ennit?"

"I'll never eat a piece of chicken again!"

And, in contradiction, "I used to like fried chicken, you know it?"

And, finally, "I can't believe I'm doing this!"

The two brothers worked quickly, then, sweating and swearing until they had looted the better share of the flock. What else were these useless, smelly creatures good for?

Dan backed the car up to the narrow door of the little shed, and they loaded the heavy sacks of chickens into the trunk, amidst loud and ongoing squawks and cries for help from the frantic birds that rang into the night.

"Hey, don't shut the lid," Dan admonished as though he

knew the protocol of chicken stealing better than his brother. "They might smother."

They went to the now-darkened house to change their clothing and wash, then, after a quick visit to the startled and puzzled Rasmussen, whom they roused from a warm bed to buy their chickens, they slipped on through the night roads. They were on their way to the Bismarck celebration, the last of the late-summer meetings of the tribes and the largest gathering of Plains dancers and singers in the north country.

In the mnemonic retelling of that long-ago event, the brothers reconciled the reverential and historical with the comic and absurd. They kept right on telling the stories as they stopped for Claude and Hosie and picked up the drum at Eagle Butte.

"Where are the chickens?" Rose Tatekeya had inquired when she returned from the hospital and the strength had come back to her body and she walked innocently around the yard. Her husband pretended that he hadn't heard, saddled up his horse, and rode over the hill.

Later, at the evening meal, however, she wouldn't be put off.

"Where are the chickens?" she insisted.

When John left the table and she had the old lady by herself, she asked again, and the old gramma finally admitted that John had sold them.

"Sold them?" Rose asked in disbelief. "But why? Who did he sell them to?"

They sat at the table in silence, each of them a little hesitant to push this inquiry any further. But Rose, being a woman of forthrightness and action, refused to accept the nonanswers she had been getting.

"What did he sell the chickens for, gramma?"

"He went to Bismarck," the old lady finally blurted. "With Dan."

Furious, Rose stormed out the door and confronted John.

"While I'm in the hospital you sell off my chickens just so that you can run around with that no-good brother of yours? What am I going to do now?"

Crying loudly and despairingly, she retreated to the house, and John walked disconsolately to the corral. Later, he accused the old lady who was a mother to him of being a troublemaker, and she packed her extra clothing in a black shawl and set out walking to her own house a mile and a half away, down on the creek. The little girls ran after her, calling, "*Unchi, Unchi.*"

They cried for her to come back, but she wouldn't listen to them this time, refusing their pleas.

On the north road to Bismarck, Dan recalled, "The old woman was eventually forced into telling the truth of it, wasn't she?"

"Yeah," said John, chuckling.

"Oh, shit!" He went on, "When Rosie got home, man, was she mad!" He shook his head as though in wonder that he'd lived to tell of it all.

"Those were the bad old days, ennit, brother?" said Dan, looking over at John, and they both, regretfully, and in hindsight, knew in their hearts that their behavior had been childish and irresponsible.

"But we were much younger then, ennit?" Smiling.

In unison, they started singing an old cowboy song: "From this valley they say we are going . . . do not hasten to bid us adieu . . ."

Claude and Hosie joined in.

19

It was Monday, the day before the beginning of the Bismarck *wacipi,* and the men who had driven through the night arrived in the city not long before the morning stars began disappearing. They drove along the outskirts to the powwow grounds, cut the engine of their vehicle, dimmed the lights, and, slumping into cramped sleeping positions in the car, dozed fitfully until the morning light.

Stars were barely visible as they slept, for the sky was becoming increasingly overcast on these near-winter days and nights. Some of the forms of life on the prairie had already started to acknowledge that they would not survive the time when the white storms would blanket the land, bearers of a cold so vicious it could crack the limbs of trees. The tree sparrows, those constant companions in such cyclical events, those survivors which nest year-round in the Northern Plains, slept in the trees hovering over the still vehicle and the men, intermittently and restlessly flitting nearby, adjusting themselves to the warmth of the flock, safe in the midst of their species. With no sense of dread, such as must be felt by those birds which had already begun to gather for their long and difficult flight to warmer climates, these drab little sparrows were the only creatures to hover near the automobile where the singers slept.

It was said that there had been, in the old days, a great Sioux trading camp near this place. In order to exchange goods at the new settlement, Indians lighted their fires near this spot when the white man first came into their country. Their children, mounted on quick ponies, played a game much like the white man's polo. And the men and women of the tribe were sometimes forced to place their dead on high scaffolds in this vicinity.

Their songs, in times of grief as well as in the time of celebration, filled the air in those days, it was said, and it may have been the spirit of that history which now held watch, as did the tree sparrows, over the men in the semi-darkness, as they slept under the nearly starless sky.

Several hundred Sioux traders lived near this spot in those previous days nearly a century before, and Tatekeya's relatives had kept those days in their memories. His great-grandmother had been among this regular nucleus of Sioux traders. She had been a young married woman at that time, just beginning her adulthood.

When the U.S. Cavalry thought that Little Thunder, the principal chief of the Platte Brules, found refuge among these people at this distant settlement following the Harney attack at Ash Hollow on the Blue Water (an unfounded rumor which was later abandoned), the soldiers burned their possessions and Tatekeya's great-grandmother's arm was ripped off at the elbow by the bullet of a soldier who had been, at one time, one of Harney's sharpshooters. After that, the woman bore seven children. She lived to a ripe old age and became unforgettable as a historian of the tribe and the possessor of a remarkable memory.

If anyone had asked, Tatekeya might have confided that the story of his great-grandmother's life here might have been one of the significant reasons for his continued annual participation in this far-north celebration; that, indeed, his own need to remember the songs that she might have sung to give strength to the people, his own wish to create new songs for the future lives of his children and grandchildren, brought him here. He placed great faith in the old songs, and he and his younger brother, Dan, knew them all.

After the traders moved from this place, it became a bivouac area for U.S. Army troops. Even later, the yellow-haired George A. Custer, the adversary of the powerful Sioux, and hero to Cunningham, Tatekeya's hapless defender-in-law, had led his unfortunate troops from this area to their deaths hundreds of miles away.

Perhaps it was some kind of perverse sense of irony which brought the modern Sioux here for the annual ceremonial, for Custer was supposed to have said, after a particularly successful prior engagement with them, "Yes. I hated to see those savage redskins killed, but it had to be done." The tellers of that tale smiled secretly. Whatever the reason, the ceremonial had the reputation of being the largest single gathering of the year for the nations of the Northern Plains. It was now like challenging an enemy, a matter of tradition, not only for the Sioux but for the Cheyennes, Crees, Chippewas, Gros Ventres, and countless other peoples. These plains Indians hosted tribes from all over the country and taught every visiting Indian singer their victory songs.

As the Tatekeya singers slept late, the silent, dark night ended with the start of a deep violet hue in the east which lasted only a few minutes, a brief breaking of the dawn which was usually witnessed by only a few of the earliest risers, a couple of old men perhaps, whose habit it was to make prayers to the sacred re-creation of the world.

The hardy sparrows began to chat as the dawn appeared, and the travelers stretched out their stiffness in the morning light, resisting the temptation to close their eyes again.

The sun rose into the sky, and they began their preparations for the dance, washing at the communal faucet, combing, brushing, and, finally, preparing the drum.

There was never a time when John Tatekeya had come to sing at the last, fall intertribal dance of the year that the bald eagles hadn't appeared, and this time was no different. First one eagle came and circled over the dance arbor as the singing started. Then another. And another. Finally, four eagles had kept watch on the singers and dancers that first afternoon. Everyone commented on the presence of the great birds, and the four men who had driven through the night welcomed the sign.

Under the arbor, the Tatekeya brothers and those who traditionally sat with them at the drum sang the song of nationhood that reminded the people of who they were and who they had always been. Old men of the tribes carrying flags, traditional female dancers, youthful fancy and shawl dancers, grass dancers — they all emerged from the entrance and formed the spectacular circles which everyone recognized as symbols of survival. The witnesses in the arbor rose up, men removed their caps, and women covered their shoulders with painted shawls. "Sh-h-h," they whispered to children.

The Tatekeya drum and the drums of all their relatives were heard all day and far into the night.

20

November 1967

The courtroom was full, and he could see the tension fade from his lawyer's face as he spied him across the crowded room. What a puzzling phenomenon, thought John, trying not to be drawn into the attorney's enthusiasm for what could be the final day of the trial. Who cares about this strange ordeal?

Perhaps, as people of the city will flock to the most talked-about movie or theater presentation, he reasoned, so do residents of a small, rural community gather for even the slightest acting-out of a resolution of conflict.

Let's get on with it, he thought, for it had all now become anticlimactic for him, and he cared little about its outcome.

John and the young Big Pipe brothers were not the only Indians present on this day, and as he looked around, John recognized others from the community: the fellow from Lower Brule who had stolen his car a couple of years ago, the act of a drunken spree that had not been so quickly forgotten; the white rancher who lived next to him and was recently reelected County Commissioner; his crippled son; several Indian women who sewed quilts at the church with Aurelia's grandmother; Clarissa; and her youngest daughter.

Even Red Hair, who had now become a spectator rather than an investigator or a witness. And many others.

John took his seat at the broad, shiny table with the District Attorney directly in front of the judge and to the center of the view of the jury. The Big Pipe brothers sat together in one of the middle rows of spectators.

The accused cattle thief sat with his counsel, Joseph Nelson III, just across the aisle, expectant, puerile. His gray-haired mother sat directly behind him.

The District Attorney began a long review of his findings and then faced the jury.

"You know," he said, "when you get right down to it, this is a case of do you believe Mr. Tatekeya was missing the cattle that he claimed he was missing at the time he claimed they were missing. Now, stop and think of that," he said carefully, summing up the case which John Tatekeya and the federal government had brought against the young white man.

"Was he missing these cattle?" he persisted.

He walked over and put his hands on the railing.

"Now, the defense of this young man here" — gesturing toward the table where the accused sat with his eyes glued to the jury box — "they claim that Mr. Tatekeya sold them himself, or he probably let them run off; that he didn't keep them fenced in and they might have just run off into the backwaters of the dam, the river, and drowned. Or they just, somehow, disappeared. Now. Stop to think of that."

The amateur historian of George Armstrong Custer paused and put his head down as though thinking about it himself for the first time.

"Now, here is a situation . . . where" — he paused — "sure, they've made him out as a heavy drinker, and apparently he likes to visit the Aurelia Blue home. And he probably wasn't there every day to watch his cattle. And he doesn't have any horses to use and he's too lazy to ride them, anyway."

He looked into the faces of the members of the jury and

fell momentarily silent. He knew that, unfortunately, they were apt to share the view presented by the accused's lawyer. All men. White men. Hard workers. They lived around Indians all their lives and did not have a good opinion of them, thinking that they were parasites on the federal government, that the BIA "took care of them." They were earnest men who slept with somber women, wives with large hips and rough complexions who turned away from them in the night. They worried about paying the bills and the price of commodities. They grieved that their children left for the cities when they grew up. And, more than most people, they believed that someone who didn't stay home and pay attention to his range work probably deserved to have his cattle stolen.

"I wonder," mused the lawyer as if to himself as he kept his eyes on the jury. He had to believe that they were fair-minded, that they could rise above their own prejudices.

"Who is on trial here? The question. Who is on trial? Who is missing these cattle? And do you think he is telling the truth? Do you believe him?"

Gesturing toward John: "There's a fellow that" — another pause — "well, he just didn't like the white man's court. It was pretty difficult for him to get up there and testify. The question is, was he telling the truth, members of the jury? Is it possible that he is telling the truth and this young man here did steal his cattle?"

The District Attorney didn't look at the short, blond young man who sat at the defense table.

"Here's a fellow, gentlemen, here's my client, Mr. Tatekeya, that was a pigeon, gentlemen of the jury. He was a sitting pigeon for this fellow here." The lawyer's arm swept toward the defendant but he still did not look at him. He kept his eyes fastened on the jury.

"This defendant knew him! Knew his operation! Knew that his place was flooded out by the dam and that he had to move his operation and that he didn't have adequate fences! Knew that he was gone sometimes! Maybe even knew *when* he was gone."

He paused for a long time.

"Knew," he said softly, "that this was a place where he could pick up cattle from an Indian who might not —"

At this point, Joseph Nelson III jumped to his feet dramatically.

"Just a moment, your honor!" he said indignantly. "I hate to object during argument, but I don't believe there's been any evidence to this effect whatsoever! It is an insult to my client."

The accused blinked toward his mother, whose stricken face turned ashen.

The judge, calm and deliberate, ruled: "Well, I think it's an inference that he may be able to use by way of argument, simply for the fact that there is testimony as to the map as to how close they live to each other. They know each other and the testimony suggests that this may be inferred. The objection is overruled. It's argument."

John looked around the courtroom. He saw the tension in the faces of the young Big Pipe brothers. He longed to see Rose's face among the spectators, some evidence of the imperturbable certitude she often shared with him and that over the years he had come to depend on. Her absence left him with a deep sense of loneliness.

He turned back to the presentation of argument.

"Just look at the kinds of things they brought into this case," the District Attorney was saying. "This is the stuff of a guilty man, to come in here and say that a man drinks too much or he is seeing a woman who is not his wife. This is absurd, and you know it and I know it. What else can a guilty man bring up but that which casts doubt on another?"

Jason Big Pipe, the young man who had testified to John's culpable behavior, got up and walked out of the courtroom. He was stopped at the door, told by the sergeant at arms that he shouldn't leave in the middle of the lawyer's presentation of argument, but he shoved his shoulder in the man's face and left.

"If they had a good defense they would come in here with a good defense," the lawyer continued, "not just, why doesn't he do this, why doesn't he do that, he should have stayed home, he should have done better.

"Gentlemen of the jury, I've seen this done many times and so have you. Especially in cattle-rustling cases. They are the toughest because you don't have a moving picture out there of people loading a truck up in a corral and trucking cattle off. This is done in the stealth of the night."

He paused to allow this imagery to be realized in the minds of the jurors.

"What kinds of witnesses were brought in? Were they reliable? Do you believe them? Or do you believe Mr. Tatekeya?

"We submit, gentlemen of the jury, that you will find that my client is telling the truth, that this young man here, sitting at this defense table, stole Mr. Tatekeya's cattle. And you should find him guilty.

"Thank you."

Part Three

A Verdict
Something Said Truly

William S. Harney

"Long Mandan said that he did not want the soldiers to go further
up the river. But the soldiers will go wherever they please. The
Great Father owns all the country, his soldiers go where they please
and take what they please, but they will always be just
to his red children."

A Report to the Proceedings, Council at Fort Pierre
March 3, 1856

21

The Last Dance Before Snow Falls

1967

The deliberations of the jury would take little more than a couple of days. At the moment of the judge's formal instructions to the jury, Aurelia was at home putting clean clothes on her grandmother following the old lady's bath. And just then, Jason Big Pipe appeared at her front door.

She looked at him, trying not to show her surprise.

"Uh . . . a . . .'*el naka' huwo,*" he said, at first. (Are you home?) Almost fearfully.

She said nothing.

Then, in English, as though he had changed his mind, "Uh . . . is your grandmother home?" he asked. Confident now.

Aurelia moved away and he stepped inside.

His eyes were on Grandmother Blue as she waddled across the room, huge and grandiose in her ankle-length black dress, so fat she required Aurelia's help to get from the bedroom to the living room couch, and as soon as she was seated, Jason went over and shook hands with her. In some kind of supplicatory way that made Aurelia turn away to conceal her scorn, he asked about the old lady's health, using the old language which he knew to be her preference.

Young men often directed what the old lady regarded as superfluous conversation and phony politeness toward her because she was the grandmother of the lovely Aurelia. Such gestures usually went unacknowledged, but this day there seemed to be a faint truce in the air, and Aurelia wondered what it all meant. The old lady smiled, uncharacteristically, but ended up simply grunting in his direction and gesturing toward her damp, tangled hair. Aurelia immediately fell to combing the long, steel-gray strands.

Jason stood awkwardly at the door until the grandmother poked Aurelia and whispered *"wakadyapi"* under her breath.

"Oh, yes. There's some coffee on the stove if you want to help yourself," Aurelia said in English as though by some vague signal she wanted him to know that she was hardly neutral or indifferent to his recent behavior.

"Thanks," he said, paying no attention to her aloof tone, glad for the chance to be in the presence of this lovely woman and show that he might be attentive.

He poured himself a cup of coffee and sat across from the grandmother, trying to ignore her unblinking stare.

"You gettin' ready to go to Fort to the dance?" he asked softly.

"Yes," said Aurelia.

"You don't need a ride, huh?"

"No, thanks."

While they carried on this harmless and stilted dialogue the old grandmother reluctantly closed her eyes and listened to the drone of their voices. Aurelia separated each strand of hair and lifted it carefully, braiding and smoothing and patting, pressing with her thumbs the limp threads of flimsy tapers, then wrapping the ends with strips of soft buckskin. She took the scarf from her grandmother's corpulent fingers, folded it, and placed it low over the old woman's forehead and tied it at the nape of her neck.

When she was finished, she poured a cup of coffee for her grandmother, who continued to doze intermittently, and one for herself and sat down, making casual conversation. No one mentioned the Tatekeya trial. Finally, when their talk dwindled to awkwardness, Jason said, "Well, maybe I'll see you at the dance," and he stepped toward the door.

Aurelia said as he left, "Maybe."

Jason noticed that the old lady's eyes were wide open, suspicious and cold.

He walked carefully down the faded wooden steps, avoiding the pail half-filled with ashes from the stove, the dog's old beef bones, the clutter. Before he left, he went over to the woodpile, picked up some chunks, and spent the next few minutes hauling stovewood up to the door, a gesture at once intimate yet generous and neighborly. He stacked it meticulously in the large wooden box at the head of the steps. Aurelia watched him from the window without expression.

As he walked to his rig, he was painfully aware that he had been treated with extreme politeness but had not been given even the slightest hint that Aurelia would be looking forward to seeing him again. She had not taken the opportunity of his visit to talk with him about his damaging testimony against John Tatekeya. And he felt that was a promising sign.

When he talked to his cousin, later, about his visit to Aurelia, and about going to the dance, his cousin said, laughing, "Hey, she's a little old for you, ennit? What? She gonna rob the cradle?"

"(K)unshi," said Aurelia, "Auntie Mart will bring NaNa, and Cecil said we could borrow his car. He should be here any minute, so hurry up." Her grandmother didn't open her eyes.

Aurelia could not remember when her grandparents had lived together. The old man, NaNa, had gone to stay with his youngest daughter, Martha, when he was only about sixty years of age. That was some time before her grandmother had taken her to raise, but Aurelia felt then, and even now in retrospect, that the two events were quite unrelated. It was not in Aurelia's memory, either, that there was any animosity between the grandmother and grandfather. The whole family adjusted easily to these changes and preferences of old age.

As she got herself ready for the dance and as her grandmother snoozed in the living room, Aurelia, in warm remembrance, thought of the time that she and John Tatekeya had gone to visit NaNa at the rest home, the time she had taken the old man some new turnips and he had sucked on them, toothlessly, while she talked to him about times past.

In response to her storytelling that day, he had begun to talk in his high, thin voice. He told her about the time he had, alone, driven twenty head of cattle from Greenwood to his parents' place along the Crow Creek at the time of his uncle's marriage and how it had rained and the leaves were golden brown. He remembered with astonishing clarity the places where he had camped and how the trees looked and which turns in the ravines were to be crossed, which to be followed. The cattle drive had taken him four days, and he hadn't eaten anything except dried meat the whole time. Packs of dried meat. *Wa co ni ca ka sa ka.*

He told her how the stars had looked and mentioned the brightest ones, saying, "Women, you know, have always been related to the stars in ways that are better than the ways of men, yes? Nevertheless, I watched them at night and knew that I would find a woman. Sometime.

"I didn't get married for a long time after those events," he mused, his tongue lisping against his sunken cheeks.

"I guess I was just not very interested in being a married man," and he laughed dryly.

"My sisters, you know," he had told Aurelia that day, "they were originally from Cheyenne River, you know. And they treated my wife very bad. And she had to put up with their insults.

"All of this was probably my fault," he went on, "because my father, who died when I was four years old, was really a more important man than their father, who had married my widowed mother. We went to live with them up at Thunder Butte. But we didn't like it there, and so we forced them all to return to our homelands at Crow Creek after the two sisters were a little older."

The whole matter, he had told her laboriously, had caused great enmity between his mother, her second husband, and his half-sisters, Corrine and Sylvia. They often claimed precedence and insisted upon making him insignificant even though his own father had been an important figure in the tribe, one who had been known for his youthful bravery during the Ghost Dance time, and one who was sent immediately to the Carlisle Indian School in the east, even before the fighting had stopped.

The visiting day, now seemingly so long ago, that she had spent with the grandfather was in her thoughts as she finished her preparations for the dance, and she was looking forward with great enthusiasm to seeing him again, listening to his songs, his stories, his prayers. The desultory tellings of stories by the old people with whom she lived informed her daily life and gave meaning to the world she knew. Such familial experience almost made Aurelia a tribal historian, though she would lay no deliberate claim to such a role. She could, however, trace with great attentiveness the important relationships, the genealogies, and the events, both historical and personal, of all those around her. And this ability was thought to be one of her special virtues, as it was always thought to be a quality of excellence in anyone who claimed to be a Dakotah.

John had sat with Aurelia and her grandfather that day far into the evening. And now, she cherished the memory of it. He has always known me, she thought. John has always known me. As much as anyone has ever known me. What will I do without him?

Assembling the family for social occasions was hard work for everyone. Clothes had to be cleaned and repaired. Children, infants, and the aged required the help of those who were mature and in good health, and so, naturally, Aurelia found herself faced with unusual responsibilities during these times.

After she had bathed, changed her clothes, and combed her hair, she awakened her grandmother, packed provisions in the car, and drove with the old lady to join the family at the Agency.

Making a right turn off the highway, Aurelia pulled the car into the grassy parking area, assisted her grandmother to the arbor to find a place to sit, and then returned to the car to get herself dressed for the dance. The grounds were filled with cars, people, a few horses, and kids of all ages everywhere. Since she was not one of the campers, she began the tedious task of pulling suitcases from the trunk and arranging her dance regalia on the front seat of the car.

As always when she prepared to dance with her relatives, she began by burning some sage and saying her prayers for making the historical past and the contemporary present significant and meaningful. This time, as she meticulously donned each article of clothing and jewelry, tied the quilled medicine wheel in her hair, put on her breastplate and adjusted it, she was aware of a feeling of anxiety she could not explain.

She walked across the grounds to her aunt Martha's old station wagon, where NaNa sat all bundled up, drinking coffee from a thermos and enjoying the crisp smell of the fall air. NaNa took the sage from Aurelia's hands, struck a match to it, and, cradling it in his hands on the small, cupped stone he carried in his pocket, helped her continue her prayers for the dancers and singers who gathered here in the old way.

Aunt Martha, not given to prayerful illumination of the deeds in one's past nor, even, in one's present, rudely grabbed some folding chairs and ushered several youngsters toward the dance area, saying, to no one in particular, "I hope he doesn't burn up the car with that," and then, "Help him over here, Aurelia."

When the old man's prayers were finished, Aurelia gave him his walking stick, and together, each thankful for the other's presence, they walked slowly, in step with one another, across the grounds and found places in the family circle to seat themselves.

They looked around to see who was present, what drums were here representing their tribes and communities, and they felt reassured that the world was right with itself. After a few moments, one of the old man's nephews came over and asked him to join the Old Agency Singers at the drum. As he did so, Aurelia and her aunt drifted toward the arbor's opening so that they could be a part of the ritualized entry from the west of the colorful procession of hundreds of dancers, filling the dance grounds as the flag songs began. At the beginning of every dance, everyone was aware that these were occasions of great importance, and they behaved with dignity and composure.

It was later, when the evening turned cold and the wind began to rise, during the hoop-dance demonstration by her aunt Martha's grandson, when she strolled casually to the car to get her grandmother's blanket to cover the old lady's knees, that she encountered Jason Big Pipe again.

"Oh, you decided to come." She pretended to be surprised, though she suddenly knew that this meeting was not a chance one. It was, in fact, what she had anticipated throughout the evening.

"Yeah," he said, smiling. "I decided that I would come for you."

Though she had heard such declarations many times before in different circumstances, she stood away from him for only a moment, and then, with the air of a woman who knew what she was doing, she put out her cigarette, twisting it carefully under her foot.

She turned to him, her face serious, luminous, and beautiful in the night shadows, and handed him her grandmother's blanket. They walked together to the dance area, but neither of them had any idea at the time how frail such moments were, nor how irrevocable.

Jason, however, who imagined himself during that moment of acquiescence better than anyone around could see him, knew that his dark eyes were filled with unaccustomed tenderness, and he felt his every step and gesture filled with confidence and faith. He gave the old grandmother a brilliant smile as he handed her the blanket to cover her lap in the evening's brittle air. He turned, then, and took Aurelia's hands in his own for a Rabbit Dance.

They are all watching, the song warned, *Pretend you don't care.* It was a lover's song, and because it was, Aurelia shaded her eyes, avoiding Jason's direct gaze as they stepped together, in time together, her arm resting lightly at his waist, in perfect cadence with the drum and the sounds of the Old Agency Singers. Their dance was full of grace, as though they had always held each other close to the heart.

Aurelia, in all the years of her youth, had never danced with John Tatekeya, for he had given it up long before he knew her. She had forgotten the playfulness, the fun of such activity, and her smile came easily as she moved in the circle with the young man who had just a few days before testified falsely against the man she had loved for so many years; the young man who had given false testimony against an important fellow tribesman in the white man's court of law; a traitor; a collaborator. There are always those among us, she thought. And we are taught to know them.

She despised his lies.

She felt his strong arms around her. Her face softened in the dimness of the night circle. Though she had always believed individual transgressions to be inexcusable and the responsibility for them unavoidable, she, at the time, listened only to the song, *pretend you don't know me.* Her face was turned away from him and she thought, He is smiling and wondering about me, just as I am wondering about him.

"You really gonna come home with me?" he asked, half in jest. Teasing, yet urgent.

She said nothing aloud but she knew, even then, that she would go with him this night. She looked over and met her grandfather's uneasy glance for just a moment. He was singing, his mouth wide open and his body shaking as his right arm came down again and again, rhythmically and surely. That song. Do I know that song?

She turned toward the place where her grandmother and all of her relatives sat beneath the arbor, and as she moved away from them in the dancers' wide circle, she wondered what they would think.

Well, they have never approved of me, she thought defiantly. Never in the past. Why should they now?

Jason caught her eye.

"I mean," he went on hesitantly, "what about . . . about . . . John Tatekeya?"

He was serious now. No longer smiling.

"You . . . ah . . . you been with him . . . a . . . long time."

The night air was turning frigid. The wind continued to rise, a signal that this last dance before winter was a prelude to the deep, heavy snowfall of a long season. Expected. Inevitable.

Yes. I have loved John Tatekeya for a long time, she remembered. All of my important years have been shared with him. I have watched with my own eyes the changes of our lives, the land. The river. And now, another betrayal. And I, too, have become a part of it.

Let me think. Don't listen to the song. Yes, it was last year at the beginning of winter that John and I began to realize we would not be exempt, that even those things that are as old as the earth itself — like honor, and virtue, and love — they are not eternal. That everything must change.

We began to know it for sure that one night. When was it? Last year? *O-hanh* . . . last year . . . about this time. We were walking the streets of Rapid City with his brother Ted, talking with him about going back for treatment to the Indian hospital: the Sioux San. That place built by the U.S. government on a hill overlooking the Rapid Creek, its long, brick driveway the path for the coming and going of its native patients as tuberculosis attacked the cell system. Silently. Surreptitiously. And it wasn't until the cough started that you even suspected its presence.

The hospital was a dreaded place which both Ted and

John saw as a place from which no one escaped. It seemed not unlike the places where the fish in the northwest rivers go to spawn. Where you go to breathe your last breath, or perform your last helpless act. The saddest place on earth.

Ted and John saw it as a place from which no one escaped. A place of death; for their youngest sister had come here in 1939 and left only when they finally put her in a wooden box. Her lungs were attacked viciously by the rod-shaped bacterium which caused the weakness and the waste in her body. But her response to the cure, her apathy and acute depression, they thought, had been as devastating as the disease itself. Their grandmother told them, ever after that, "It's where they take you to die."

Ted made several Peyote songs to sing for her recovery. Yet Sister gave up her life in this world, saying only, "You must try to remember me." She was, at the time of her death, thirty-two years old, and her babies, without her, were forever quiet and forlorn.

Instead of returning to the hospital, Ted drank steadily, his bottle of Ten High in the pocket of his heavy sheepskin coat, which, unzipped, flapped into the bitter wind. His clumsy movements made him seem to lunge, again and again, into the wind as we paced the streets, as though:

> The world he lived in
> was like some vast museum with rock walls
> but lifeless as artifact,
> cellophaned, preserved. He put
> great faith in the holy men who sang
> to hailstones because, he said, there
> are four posts holding up the Earth,
> and four beavers busily gnawing
> at each.
>
> He lived in the museum of rock walls,
> paleolithic and alone, habitually ascetic,
> questioning the reliability
> of messages from curators
> only recently revealed. Fraudulent.

Capricious. Their imaginary
lives and deaths encompassed his misery.

Eventually, he became the man who walked
into the day, following a ditch
along a country road so luminous
he couldn't find his way home. Heat from
the glossy rocks on this isolated country road
marred his forehead and cheek, and when the others
found him, he was too weak to breathe,
supine, and covered with dust.

Because we were nearly broke, I went into a coffee shop across from Duhamels' to see if there might be somebody who would buy some of my beaded jewelry. Just a few doors down, there was a hock shop, but I didn't know that until later when it really didn't matter anymore. I sat down and stared at myself in the mirror across the counter. My eyes, narrow and black, like solitary, distant crescents in a brilliant mask, shaded my misery. And I looked, I thought, like I was all right.

"What'll you have?"

I pulled out a sparkling, beaded hairpiece from my purse and held it idly.

"You wanna buy this?"

"Chrissakes! What would I do with that?"

I looked up and, for the first time, focused upon the woman's weary sallowness. It was the face of a person whose passion for life was all undone, after years and years of solemn, unhappy survival.

"Oh, well . . . yes . . . ," I said uncertainly.

I put the brilliant hairpiece back in my purse and moved toward the door.

"Well, what do you want? Don't you wanna order nothin'?"

The woman threw her order pad on the counter in disgust, and I escaped through the heavy doors.

John turned his back to me as we slept that night in a seedy motel, lights flickering and wheels grinding, as trucks met the stoplights just a few feet from the motel courtyard. Ted sat in a chair, coughing up spittle throughout the night, and by morning was running a mortal fever.

We had no heater in our car but drove back to the Agency anyway, over two hundred miles, with Ted asleep in the backseat, burning up with a deathly high temperature, his lips parched and swollen. When we got there, they told us that we should take him to Chamberlain, to the white man's hospital about twenty miles away, a place where Indian patients are sometimes treated in emergency cases.

Ted died that night, during the first snowfall of the season, just before his son arrived from Fargo.

As we walked out of the waiting rooms, John said to me in Indian, "Ah, the grandfather has come," and for just a brief moment, I had no idea what he meant. Then he held out his hand to catch the falling snow, and for the first time in days, he seemed to relax and give in to the whims and absurdities and inevitabilities of our lives.

As I think of it all now, as I look back on it, I know that we both sensed that it was, as John said, "all going to hell."

The song ended and Jason and Aurelia walked out of the arbor to the foodstands which rimmed the dance area. They walked the circle several times to make sure that they were seen by everyone who mattered; then they sat down to a serious conversation at one of the picnic tables. He brought her a steaming cup of coffee and she began:

"John Tatekeya is a man of the past." She smiled wistfully. "A man who has taught me everything.

"He could not predict the theft," she said defensively. "Nor the betrayal. But when it happened he knew that it was the changing of the river that accounted for his dilemma. Even though it started long ago."

Jason sat without looking at her, his fingers curled around the warm cup.

"It was the river. . . ." Her voice trailed off and was lost, momentarily, in the wind.

Jason said nothing.

"He used to listen to me talk about my mother's ways, her new ways" — she paused — "and he used to tell me it was all going to hell. The flooding of his place. It made everything for him distorted. Strange.

"Finally," she said in a low voice, "he became very angry about the trial. The stupid trial. And he doesn't quite know what to do."

It was the first time that she mentioned the trial, and Jason held his breath.

"He doesn't know, really, what to do," she repeated.

"And neither do you," Jason said, his voice rising as if he had asked a question.

The cold wind began to whip around her legs and she covered them with her shawl. She looked up at him and shrugged.

He waited for her to speak.

At last she said, "And you?"

People were beginning to head for their cars to get their coats and blankets. Even a few of the dancers, carrying feather-bustles and suitcases, strolled through the circle taking a final look at the display of wares as the evening's activities seemed to be drawing to an untimely close while the weather worsened. Dust, brittle leaves, empty paper cups, and other trash from the foodstands swirled about the grounds.

Reluctant to leave this last dance of the year, people stood around in small clusters, talking quietly. Waiting for the inevitable wind to turn to sleeting rain. They pulled their wraps closer.

"He always told me, you see, Jason" — she sounded like a mother talking to a recalcitrant child — "that you don't accomplish anything in life for personal and individual reasons alone."

"But, yeah," Jason interrupted. "Sure. I believe that, too."

"That all accomplishments and events and doings" — she swung her arm widely — "must contribute in a good way to the communal life given to us by our ancestors."

"Yeah," said Jason, nodding his head.

As though she hadn't heard his agreement, she mused, "And the river was always a part of . . . a part of . . . and the land . . .

"But, now, you see . . ." Her words again drifted away in the wind.

She left unsaid what they both knew: that her own relationship with Tatekeya as well as the ugly testimony given by Jason at the trial had successfully shifted the guilt of the white man's theft to the people, *Oyate,* to themselves and each other and all who clung tenaciously to the notion that, even amidst devastating change, the Dakotahs were people who were obliged to be responsible to one another.

This has always been true, she thought. Always. Until . . .

As the two talked into the darkness, mindless of the rising night wind, they began to feel better. What can we do, they asked one another. They held each other's hands and they began to understand. Nothing lives long, and it is only the tribes and the land that continue.

At last, Jason stood up and said gently, "Come on. Let's go. We must take your grandmother home."

To Aurelia he seemed very tall, and she no longer thought of him as a boy. He stuffed one hand in the pocket of his jeans, put the other around her shoulders, and they walked silently away from the lighted dance area into the darkness.

Jason felt Aurelia's small hand at his waist, and he listened to the long strands of beads echoing in perfect rhythm against the bone of the breastplate she wore. The fringes of her shawl swung up and down as they walked together, and Jason knew that there would be no moments so sweet as this. They had danced together this night, and it was the first time that he had touched her, and he was dazzled.

"We,
    the Jury,

Find the defendant guilty of the crime of stealing
personal property of a value exceeding $100 on the Crow Creek
Indian Reservation from Mr. John Tatekeya, an Indian,
as charged in the indictment."

Late fall, 1967

22

In the aftermath of the trial no one knew quite what to expect, and they mostly went about their private ways.

While the lawyers went on to other cases in their continuing pursuit of justice, the litigants and spectators took up their lives, and the trial's end and the days after the verdict were much like any other endings and all days for many of them. For Tatekeya, however, the world was changed forever.

In his own first thoughts concerning the events of the past several months, he felt: *he mac 'ena* (I am still the same). But, of course, he was not. And in his heart he knew better. His life was changed irrevocably just as the river had been changed for all eternity.

He drove to the Joe Creek at the West End of the reservation immediately after the verdict was read and the court dismissed, then followed the gravel road around the bend in the river. He stopped and parked his vehicle at the small U.S. government–installed boat dock without speaking to anyone, arriving there just before sundown.

He sat for a long time with the pickup door open and the chilly wind whipping at his legs. There were great ponderous waves on the gray water. They seemed to come from its depths, and, looking at the phenomenon with great interest, John remembered the stories about the remarkable *unktech-ies* who, at the beginning of time, ripped off first one arm and then the other and flung them into the water. One was a female figure and the other a male. They taught the Indians what they needed to know about religion, and, it was said, they subsequently went deep into the earth themselves. *"They are still there,"* the old people would say. *"Waiting and listening for the prayers of Indians. They are listening to hear the drums of Indians."*

That's what Benno used to tell me, thought John as he looked without emotion into the rough, wind-driven waves. He remembered, too, how he had walked to his mailbox in water up to his knees when the water seeped in, higher and higher every day, when part of his lands were flooded. One day, the road was still there and the mail carrier drove his vehicle on his appointed rounds, and the next day, the road was under water. It was just before the men came up from the Agency and moved his little house out of the way of the vast destruction. His youngest daughter had been with him and he had consoled her panic, though he had felt it, too, as they and others from the community watched from the hills.

At last, sitting slumped in his pickup, he knew that he would not be among those who were driven from this land by such violence. He knew that he would stay here. Die here. Because of the *unktechies*. Because of Benno. This thoughtful assurance brought him some measure of peace.

And he knew he was not alone. He remembered with pride the efforts of John One Child, that old Santee who was more than ninety years old now, and how he came to the Council chambers last September with a small request; a request which was, in John's mind at least, emblematic of the tenacity with which Dakotahs faced such brutality. Yes. It was just about the time that the trial started. And One Child asked that the lake which had been formed at the bend in the river be named Dakotah Lake. For the people. Rather than Lake

Marcus in honor of the old lawyer and politician named M. Q. Marcus, a white man who had participated in the litigation by the federal government and "sold out" the tribe for four hundred dollars per capita.

It was One Child's second request for the name change, but nothing could be done, he was told. The Agency, you see, he was told, had already celebrated its one-hundredth birthday. Its centennial. Back in 1963. And so, you see, he was told, there would be no occasion for changing the name at this time. John's mouth turned down in a sardonic smile.

Tatekeya turned in his seat and looked out across the road at the land which he and his people had called their own even before the Indian Reorganization Era forced them into individual ownership. It was Dakotah land which he and the others had defended all their lives in ways that ordinary people could not imagine, against theft and fraud and exploitation of every sort. Sometimes they were successful. Sometimes not. He remembered the gardens they used to plant along the river there. Every summer. The good sweet corn and the squash.

Back at the time of his birth, just prior to the turn of the century, the beef cattle industry had become a major economic force after white men found out what the Plains Indians had probably known all along, that beef cattle would not only survive the hard winters of the north along this river, but actually thrive on the northern prairie grasses.

And soon after, as the white man continued to bargain for the land from indigenous peoples, who resisted in their desire to save their own lifeways, the exploitive and brutal policy of colonialism, a deeply felt impulse of the European newcomers, became a powerful force, at once legalized in the courts and yet denied in history.

In a few brief, hurried decades, John thought, we made unbelievable adjustments. We knew, better than most, perhaps, that new nations rise out of the blood of other nations. And we therefore changed our lives over and over again so that we would not die. Even as we dealt with the Americans, though, we never expected that we would become beggars. We never expected, as Europeans continued to leave their native countries for this land, as they made contracts with us in order to satisfy their needs, that it was their desire to manifest total authority over the vast rich lands of our fathers. My Sioux relatives, John thought, had always had confidence that no one who faced the providential spirits of the land could be so arrogant.

Finally, we have come to understand the force that we are up against, he thought with a sigh.

John returned his gaze to the water and watched its energy wane as the sun fell behind the purple hills and the wind ebbed. He watched it without thought, without emotion, without despair or panic. As darkness fell, he slumped in the front seat of his pickup and slept.

At sunrise the wind had blown itself out, and Tatekeya drove back to town to his daughter's house. His wife, Rose, met him in the yard, and she put her arm around his waist and hooked her fingers in his belt and walked slowly with him into the house. They stood inside the door, the strong sunlight slanting in the windows, and held on to one another; and he knew that while he stood accused of many things by others, of adultery, foolishness, of malice, and deceit, and theft, this woman would say that none of it carried as much weight as the years they had given to each other.

One time, when they were just children together, probably no more than nine or ten, Rose had told him a secret. She said that the cottonwood tree, the sacred tree that is used at the Sun Dance, holds inside of it the perfect five-point star.

"How do you know that?" he challenged.

The next time her older brother and the others cut down a tree for the secret ceremony and put a crosswise cut in one of the upper limbs, the two children crept in beside it, and when they looked at it, awed and hushed, they saw the whitened star, a direct link to the time when the Sioux were the Star People.

She hadn't been able to resist. "I told you so," she had said gleefully.

He had chased her home that day, angry and jealous of the secrets she knew.

Now, at the kitchen table, Rose poured hot coffee into two cups and placed one in front of John, taking the other for herself, and they began to speak, unaccountably, of the distant past. And they began to laugh together, and they laughed until tears came into their eyes and neither of them could say anything more.

John looked into the anguish in this woman's face, the furrows deep across her brow, and he knew that her laughter was a spontaneous release of tension and anxiety brought about by the events of the last days. His marriage to Rose had been one of the last arranged unions in the old *tiospaye* tradition, the last in both of their families to be given cultural sanction, and he knew that neither of them would let go of it.

He could still recall the approbation and endorsement of family members toward them. The gift giving and the feasting. The praise and flattery that had given way over the years to a devotedness and cordiality that was often taken for granted.

After a few minutes they regained their composure, and John said to Rose, "I have no cattle returned to me."

"Yes." She nodded. "I know. That is the white man's law."

They sat in silence.

"There was that old *tōka'* woman," Rose began. "Do you remember her? She was very tall and always wore long, black dresses. And the kids used to be afraid of her. Do you remember her? No one knew where she came from, but her brother lived there on the Crow Creek. They used to think that maybe she was Oglala."

John said nothing.

"I remember how she used to tell us that there is nothing we can count on, nothing in this world we can depend upon.

Don't you remember how she used to talk about how it is that the Dakotahs turn around and around and see nothing on the horizon? We can turn around and around, she told us, and look in all directions, and never even see a tree. In some places, you know. We, then, see nothing on the horizon."

"H-un-m."

"That it is . . . as though, after all, only the wind is the source of thought and behavior. The wind moves. And it is a determinant, yes?"

She wanted him to respond.

"The white man doesn't know these things, and so he always believes that his solution is significant," she went on. It was as if she had to explain to John that it was nothing new to them that the white man's law was ineffectual.

"I don't know why they sometimes called her Saul woman. She was not a Christian, I think."

When he said nothing, she said at last, "If we expect something else I think that we will be disappointed."

Instead of joining in on this focus of the discussion, John said quietly, "People know me here. They know that I have never tried to be something other than what I am."

As he sat watching her pack into laundry baskets the clothes and food that she would need so that she could drive out to the reservation with him, he began to dread the aftermath of this trial. For while Rose spoke of the failure of the white man's law, she said nothing about what they knew to be of paramount importance, the failure of reciprocity among the relatives.

What Aurelia had meant to her husband would never be asked about nor commented upon by this woman who had the ability to know secrets, the ability to distinguish between matters which are merely profoundly serious and those which are tragic. The sons of Harvey Big Pipe had directed hostile acts toward this good relative, John Tatekeya, with apparent deliberation and reason. And what this meant to all of them was that such a transformation of Dakotah values might progress, unfortunately, to somewhere outside of history. To the end of time.

"Are you ready to go?" he asked.

"Yes."

They both felt uneasy and uncertain as they drove home. Afterwards, whenever they spoke of this uneasiness they could never be sure of its cause. Had it been something between them or had it been something else, a premonition perhaps?

As they drove around the last curve within sight of the river, they saw the smoke rising and at first thought it was coming from that old, abandoned Standing place, but as they drew closer, their worst fears were realized. The makeshift trailerhouse on their place that was filled with hay was ablaze, and both of them knew that the fire would spread in a few minutes to the dozen or so haystacks set close together in the feedlot.

They raced to the scene and John stopped the pickup, leapt out, and shouted to Rose to drive quickly to the Community Center where she could use the telephone to call everyone in the neighborhood to come and help.

As she pulled out of the yard, she saw Guy LaPlant's pickup careening up to the gate.

"I seen the smoke," he hollered. "Where's John?"

She gestured toward the shed where John was already pulling around the tractor and disk, getting ready to shove dirt between the trailerhouse and the haystacks.

"Kennie's coming with his backhoe," said Guy.

Rose pulled out of the yard, scattering dirt and gravel with the wheels of the pickup.

Waves of heat swept into the dismal sky, and the yellow-gray smoke filled the lungs of the men who fought the blaze, which left behind only the outlines of charred posts and barbed wire and a large scorched circle on the earth for a quarter-mile radius. Faces blackened, their clothes torn and filthy, John and the small gathering of his neighbors sat or stood in clusters, too exhausted to speak, their lungs seared, their throats too charred and dry to breathe. Only after it was all done did the fire truck from the Agency arrive, and then two young men numbly hosed the embers with water.

To the west the grove of elm and oak which John planted two years prior to the flooding of the banks of the Missouri stood as weary sentinels, reluctant witnesses untouched by the conflagration, their leaves swept away in the wind. The house, untidy and remote, a few yards beyond the stand of trees, was undamaged by the fire.

As their energies returned, the firefighters began to drift toward the porch to commiserate with Rose and members of the family, who stood solemnly, dry-eyed.

"That didn't take long, did it, John?" said Guy, echoing his despair against the wretchedness felt by everyone.

"No. Twelve stacks and a shed full of hay . . . it don't take long to burn when there's a little wind."

They found places to sit on the wide southern porch. Some went to the pump and hauled pails and basins of water and, unmindful of the cold, began washing their faces and arms. Pretty soon they were drinking coffee, and Rose was making fry-bread. The sun went behind the hills and the exhausted little group sat in the cold shadows.

"Guy," said John softly, "tell me what you think started all this."

He was speaking philosophically about the flooding of his lands, the disappearance of life forms along the river, the trial and subsequent fire, the historical thefts of land from his people, and the agony of existence without the support of Benno. In his thoughts were the words of Gray Plume and all of the grandfathers who had said that life in accordance with the white man's ways was indecent:

> I am an Indian but the man then told me I would become an American. . . . Now, listen to what the Great Father says. . . . Harney himself had massacred the Sicangu. . . . I am not going to beg for my life . . . the soldiers go where they please. . . .

Guy, being a literal and fundamental sort, replied, "That's one thing I'm sure about . . . but we'll never prove it."

"What do you mean?"

"I'll tell you what he means." Jason Big Pipe spoke from

the darkness of the porch. John hadn't seen him come during the excitement of the fire but looked at him at that moment, his long hair streaked with mud, eyes reddened by the smoke. And with great relief he acknowledged that Jason had been there with them to fight the fire.

"That son-of-a-bitch was out on bail before you got out of the courthouse, John."

"Yeah? But . . . how?"

"His mother and his uncle showed up and paid the bail, and they've started an appeal already."

"But . . . would he do this?" John gestured toward the ruins of the trailerhouse.

"Why not? He stole your cattle," Jason said bitterly.

No one spoke in the silence that followed this angry remark, and John felt the hollow inside his chest start to burn as if from some terrible wound.

Finally John asked tiredly, "If you knew this, Jason, what the hell were you doing testifying against me?"

"He paid Sheridan to help him load that night, and I was coming home from town late and saw them. When I confronted Sheridan he said that he'd beat the shit out of me if I didn't lie for them."

Through clenched teeth and fighting back tears, he finished the story. "And, hell, I couldn't let my brother go to the pen, could I?"

Suddenly, the hollow in John's chest seemed to cave in and he couldn't breathe. He gasped and coughed. He coughed until he thought he would vomit, and he stood up and walked out to the gate. His body shook and he took great gulps of air. At last the spasm left him and he went into the house and took a long drink of cool water. He sat down in an easy chair in the living room and let the tensions loosen from his body. He felt his thoughts drift. My children were born here, right here in this room, he thought. Is that why I had the house moved to this place when my land was flooded? Where is the horse, Red Hand Warrior, that Chunskay broke to ride?

He saw Aurelia and she was crying. He repeated the words

that she had told him: *"They said that to pray to the east, south, west, north"* — and he saw her motioning — *"was to pray to the winds. And it was therefore evil."* I have nothing, he thought. Nothing is mine. And there is nothing that I can take with me when I see Benno again.

The firefighters and neighbors sitting on the porch soon began to leave, one by one, to return to their homes. Jason stayed and Rose gave him another cup of coffee, but even he, after a while, left.

When Rose went into the house she found John sitting quietly. She touched his arm. He put his hand on her hair and awkwardly smoothed it.

"I have no memory of ever wanting to hurt you," he told her.

Weeping quietly, she said. "I believe you."

"We are the children of Gray Plume," he said slowly, his head resting on the back of the chair, his eyes closed. He said it in confidence. Not in defeat or sorrow, but matter-of-factly.

23

Aurelia heard about the fire almost before the last ember had grown cold. Though she and her grandmother saw the smoke from their place, they paid scant attention until one of the white women from the church stopped by to leave a sack of old clothes from which Mrs. Blue usually cut the bright squares and triangles for her quilts.

"Tatekeya's barn was leveled by fire," the woman rasped. "But I guess they've got it out by now."

Neither Aurelia nor her grandmother responded, but Aurelia felt the slow pangs of desolation in her heart when she heard the news, and she thought immediately that this destruction would be the last of the undeserved events that John would endure. She knew that from this time on, his discontent would be equal to hers, and he would never again ask for her love.

"They are saying," the church woman went on, "that there might be something suspicious about it."

There are some people in this world who are born old, NaNa used to tell her. And Aurelia knew that she was one of those. Perhaps it was that quality which accounted for her long-standing feelings for Tatekeya, the love she had felt for him the first time he'd touched her shoulder as they'd left the church meeting together that day so long ago.

Now that the trial was over amidst the gossip that a deliberate arson might have occurred within hours of the verdict, Aurelia was forced to reach some conclusions about the situation. She reasoned that John's natural reclusiveness would become more profound, that his habitual tendency toward isolation would be intensified. He would now become a man less broadly involved in the sphere of human concerns. She knew that, now, his admiration for her would become a part of his past and his manner toward her stilted and unnatural.

She would therefore have to live her life without him for the first time in years. Her loneliness for him would be unimaginable, she feared. But she would be able to accept his absence, sooner or later, as all people are able to sustain grief and loss.

These were Aurelia's thoughts as she contemplated the very recent happenings, but she shared them with no one. From now on, she thought, she would have to pretend that she was unafraid. The trial and the fire, events which seemed to be, in her mind, as inevitable as any of the events that she had ever witnessed, rendered the questions which she and John had posed together irrelevant. She determined that she would cling no longer to the notion that the lofty ideals of her ancestors could confirm and encourage her spirit.

Because the questions no longer mattered, Aurelia felt calm and poised. As she leaned forward into the bathroom-door mirror she could see herself in the dimness . . . a pretty girl, thin, not very tall, looking years younger than her thirty-odd years, her silky hair falling to the middle of her back. Her eyes, though, her eyes . . . she leaned closer . . . black, liquid . . . eyes that barely revealed her lifelong melancholy, her new fears, her present pain, all the result of her recognition that the life which she now re-created in quick, blurry scenes of the last decade or so was to change forever. *I had to grow up and I do not regret anything.* As she turned, she seemed not to care that the deceptiveness of her youth had been dangerous and destructive, and she grabbed a sweater from the closet.

The significance of the traditional past, she knew now, was only a personal and individual matter, not consanguineous as she had supposed. Thus her mother's abandonment of tradition was her own business, and the effect such an action might have on family and tribe was worth examining only if it could make a difference. With this cynical and pragmatic recognition suddenly and profoundly thrust upon her, she knew, finally, what it meant to be alone. Even Jason, whose smile had tempted her that night, whose laughter and passion haunted her even now, could make no difference.

Aurelia stood in the darkened hallway and listened to the church woman drone endlessly as she took each piece of used clothing from the sack and remarked upon its virtues and possibilities. Her grandmother's occasional murmur did nothing to assuage the tremendous ache in her heart. From now on, now that she could no longer depend upon anyone to accept the way she was, and the way she wanted to be, and the way she had always been with Tatekeya, she would have to pretend that she was vital and that she loved life. In her future relationships with men she would have to think of ways that she might tempt them and keep them from looking at other women. She would have to force herself to seem loving and happy. And the artless beauty she had possessed so impudently all those years might now become useful as it has always been useful to women of contemporary worlds.

When the church woman drove away, and her grandmother began to talk about the cutting of quilt designs, the young grief-stricken woman turned and left the house. She felt tears fill her eyes, and as her grandmother watched from the window, she leisurely saddled her horse and rode toward the river. She looked upon the dead and dying whitened trees along the banks and knew that in spite of the river's grotesque new image and what it meant to the uncharted future, she would constantly have to remind herself of her disavowal of its avuncular nature. It would take great discipline. For here, in this place which represented the cyclical dramas of her people's past, it seemed certain that the wretchedness inflicted upon human beings by other human beings was inseparable from the violation of the earth. And only here, only now, at this time, did she take comfort in the knowledge that she was no longer completely isolated from the secret that human beings are capable of violent and destructive malice, and she was pleased in the knowledge that she would no longer ask futile questions.

She knew now that the flooding of the homelands had to be taken into account in any explanation of her devotion to Tatekeya, and his to her; that chance would have played only a slight role in such an important matter. As she looked at the waste along the edge of the endless gray water, she saw the outlines of many tipis, a village which had once stood on these inundated grounds. In the haze, horses bearing youthful riders, horses pulling travois, children and mothers carrying colorful shawls, walked slowly toward her. A slow-motion montage of all things past and eternal, unassuming and habitual, came toward her and passed over her in an indistinct white fog. It was an abstraction which moved toward the purple hills, a fleeting moment of thought to make nothing of, for it was a materialization, she knew, rising out of her grief.

John would be gone from her now, and the questions of what their lives had meant to each other as great changes occurred would not need further speculation. There would be no one else to understand that the love of her parents and grandparents, and the love of those for whom she cared deeply, and even the unalterable devotion of a lover or husband, would not make her happy. Nor would it give her peace, seize her soul, satisfy her intellect. No one but John had discovered this about her nature.

It had taken a long time, but finally she had become convinced that the reality of her mother's abandonment and the questions concerning it were futile, meant only to make her forever sad. Worst of all, she now began to accept as fact what she had always suspected, that the stories of the pipestone quarries of her people were apocryphal. Like the sacred grounds of Palestine, they could no longer symbolize the final restoration in the modern world.

She felt herself at the edge of sobs, deep and terrible. Headed north, a sudden wind hurting her nostrils, she stood up in the stirrups and held the reins high, taut. She drove her horse up a stony hill and when she got to the top, the wind, unaccountably, stilled . . . *ma tuki* . . . the horses in the adjoining pasture looked at her and the stallion flattened his ears.

As Aurelia moved on, the sky in the west turned crimson and gray as though a storm were trying hard to get started. In the dark of this night, the first of the winter snows would blanket the earth, confirming their own inevitability. The hills above the Missouri River would become white and unfathomable, secret in their private subterfuge, preoccupied and selfish in their knowledge.

An ageless gray owl turned its head toward her as she moved effortlessly along the river's edge.

Epilogue

The Afterpart

As the hide was placed over the opening, Tatekeya let his head drop to his chest in the darkness and he gripped his arms tightly around himself. Sweat poured from his body and his agony seemed interminable.

He moaned and silently wept.

As he began to sing, he lifted his head and thrust it back against the curve of the lodge. His eyes, wide open in the total darkness, looked upon the antiquities of the universe and his mind adjusted itself, by degrees, to his own triviality.

He turned toward young Philip, who put the sage carefully into the trembling hands of his venerable grandfather, Harvey Big Pipe.